Santa  or some way for Louis's words to make sense.

Marry him!

But of course, he was her, trying to punish h problem of her makin

"Good idea," she snapped. "Why don't we fly to Vegas? We could get married with Elvis as the celebrant and afterward we could invite all our new *paparazzi* friends to the reception."

His face hardened. "If you like, although I thought the whole point of getting married was to get them off our backs."

She felt her face dissolve, her mouth forming an O of shock. He was being serious.

"Are you out of your mind?"

Marry Louis: the idea was absurd and wrong on so many levels, and yet she couldn't stop a hectic pulse from leapfrogging across her skin or deflect a sudden, vivid memory of the moment when his mouth had fused with hers.

"No!" Shaking her head to clear the image, she took a step backward. "I wouldn't marry you if my life depended on it."

"What about your reputation?"

Louise Fuller

—

THE CHRISTMAS SHE MARRIED THE PLAYBOY

ISBN-13: 978-1-335-56821-2

The Christmas She Married the Playboy

Harlequin Enterprises ULC
22 Adelaide St. West, 40th Floor
Toronto, Ontario M5H 4E3, Canada
www.Harlequin.com

Printed in U.S.A.

Louise Fuller was a tomboy who hated pink and always wanted to be the prince—not the princess! Now she enjoys creating heroines who aren't pretty pushovers but are strong, believable women. Before writing for Harlequin, she studied literature and philosophy at university, then worked as a reporter on her local newspaper. She lives in Royal Tunbridge Wells with her impossibly handsome husband, Patrick, and their six children.

Books by Louise Fuller

Harlequin Presents

Craving His Forbidden Innocent
The Rules of His Baby Bargain
The Man She Should Have Married
Italian's Scandalous Marriage Plan
Beauty in the Billionaire's Bed

Passion in Paradise

Consequences of a Hot Havana Night

The Sicilian Marriage Pact

The Terms of the Sicilian's Marriage

Visit the Author Profile page
at Harlequin.com for more titles.

CHAPTER ONE

'EXCUSE ME, YOUR GRACE, I'm sorry to bother you—'

'Then don't.' Eyes shut, Louis Albemarle, Tenth Duke of Astbury, burrowed away from the steward's coaxing voice, pulling the quilt over his floppy brown hair.

'But, Your Grace—'

'Is the plane on fire?' Louis muttered irritably, shifting onto his side.

'No, sir.'

'Have the wings dropped off?'

'No, sir.'

Opening his eyes, he winced into the light, pain blooming inside his head. He glared at the steward. 'Then why have you woken me up? I said I didn't want breakfast. I said I didn't want to be woken until we got to Zurich.'

The steward nodded soothingly. 'We are in Zurich, sir. We just touched down a moment ago.'

Touched down? Surely they couldn't be here already? It felt as if he'd just put his head on the pillow. In fact, it felt as if his head *was* a pillow. And he couldn't seem to feel his jaw...

'Right. Fine. Whatever.' Holding up his hands to fend off any further interaction, he rolled onto his back. 'Just give me a minute—'

As he watched the steward retreat, Louis ran a hand over his face, the rough skin on his fingers snagging on the two-day stubble. Even the tiniest movement made him feel as if rocks were rolling around inside his head, but he just wanted to make sure his face was still there.

He stifled a yawn. Actually, what he really wanted to do was sleep for about a hundred years.

The last seven days had been another lost week of non-stop partying. Behind closed doors, so it should stay under the radar.

Not that he cared what people thought, but it just meant his voicemail wouldn't get filled up with messages bleating about his behaviour from the Callière chief marketing officer Nick Cooper.

Messages that he simply deleted.

His lip curled. Why the hell would he take any notice of them? Nobody told him how to behave in private or in public, and that included his CMO and the shareholders.

Stretching an arm over his shoulder, he swung his legs out of bed and began dragging on last night's clothes.

What he needed was a long, hot shower, and then he was going to take a sleeping pill and crash. With any luck he'd wake up just in time for the Christmas party at the Haensli—the legendary Christmas party at the equally legendary and jaw-droppingly exclusive Hotel Haensli in Klosters. It was the grandest ski palace in the Alps, and it was the one party his CMO had given the green light for.

Understandably. It was like a festive and infinitely more fun version of a Davos forum. One night when an extraordinary roster of billionaires and global aristocrats joined a dazzling guest list of big names from the entertainment world to play.

In other words, the kind of people who should and did wear Callière jewellery—which was why they were gifting each female guest a pair of diamond earrings in the lavish goodie bag.

It had been a last-minute idea—*his*, of course. But the shareholders had loved it. So would the guests.

His mouth twisted. So maybe for the first time in three months his business would be making headlines for the right reasons, and he might finally be one step closer to being able to own the business entirely.

But first he had to get to the hotel.

After the warmth of Abu Dhabi, the crisp Alpine air made his eyes water. He hunched his shoulders against the chill, a beanie pulled low over his forehead, his blue eyes hidden behind a pair of ludicrously expensive vintage sunglasses.

Not that he needed to worry about being recognised. This terminal was for private charters only. There were no commercial flights, and that meant no nosey holiday-makers with smartphones looking to make a quick buck with a photo of some celebrity tumbling off a plane.

It was why he always travelled first class.

But nothing beat a private jet for…well, for keeping your private life private. And, frankly, he needed to lie low right now, so when Henry had offered him the use of his jet, naturally he had jumped at the chance.

Unfortunately, even a private jet could only take him

so far. This next part of the journey had to be done by helicopter.

Ah, there it was: his ride.

He greeted the pilot and climbed into the sleek black helicopter. This time the flight took just over half an hour and, resisting the urge to sleep, Louis stared down at the picture-book snow-covered serenity of the Swiss Alps.

It reminded him of Canada, the place he'd called home for the last ten years. But even though he loved the endless expanse and wild beauty of Alberta and the Northwest Territories, it was not his home.

For him, that could only ever be Waverley.

And yet even now, when he could reasonably claim the house and the estate back as his own, he hadn't done so. He wasn't sure if he ever would.

His father's death should have been like a door closing. Or was it a weight lifting? He stared moodily through the window, twin pulses of resentment and bitterness beating across his skin as they always did whenever he let himself think about his parents and their actions.

Their betrayal.

Instead, his father's death had seemed to unleash a kind of fury in him that couldn't be satisfied—along with two other emotions, both of which were entirely unwelcome: guilt and regret.

Maybe it had been the shock of realising that he was now the Duke of Astbury, with the title of the man he'd spent so long hating, but all the old demons had awoken, together with a few new ones, and he'd basically spent the last three months partying so hard he couldn't stand, much less think about the past.

At Davos, a text from Henry and a flurry of snowflakes greeted him as he walked towards the heliport terminal.

No doubt Henry Sr was giving his son a hard time for handing over the family jet, but Henry Jr owed him big-time for what had happened in Cannes in the summer, so now they were quits.

A muscle twitched in his jaw. A lot of people owed him for what happened in Cannes, but as usual he'd taken the blame.

Why wouldn't he?

It wasn't as if he had a reputation to lose, he thought, his lip curling as he sidestepped a young couple kissing passionately.

He might run one of the most successful, sustainable and ethical diamond businesses in the world, but if everything he read in the media was to be believed, that was the only ethical thing in his life.

Or at least that was what most people seemed to think. Including—unfortunately, but not that surprisingly—those closest to him.

His shoulders tensed.

It had taken ten years, but Callière had gone from being a niche diamond mining and retail business to a sought-after cult jewellery brand favoured by A-listers across the planet.

He had made that happen.

It was his company, his brainchild. He was the CEO and soon the business that bore his beloved grandmother's name would be fully under his control and he would be able to forget all about the damn shareholders and their concerns.

He felt a sharp needle of resentment between his ribs.

It wasn't fair that he had been put in this position in the first place. He was the Duke of Astbury. He shouldn't have had to borrow money and he shouldn't have needed to. But there had been no alternative after his father had cut off his allowance.

If Glamma hadn't helped him he wouldn't have had anything. Not even a roof over his head.

Across the concourse the scent of hot coffee was a welcome, enticing distraction from the well-trodden path of his thoughts, and he was turning unthinkingly towards the low-lit luxurious lounge area when his brain did an emergency stop, closely followed by his feet.

Only why?

It was just a woman, wearing a white fur Cossack-style hat, with some kind of pastry in her hand, standing next to a trolley full of luggage. A lot of luggage, admittedly, but not enough to snag his gaze and hold it captive.

No, that would be her legs.

His pulse ticked.

Sheathed—and that was the only word for it—in form-hugging dark jeans, they seemed to go on for ever. Or at least to where a frustratingly obscuring navy puffer jacket skimmed over the mouthwatering curve of her bottom.

Damn. He felt his blood divert sharply to his groin and for a moment he forgot to breathe as his eyes locked on to her bottom. And now that he was looking it was almost impossible to look away. Impossible not to wonder what else lay beneath that stupid jacket. Could the rest of her be as tempting?

At that exact instant, the woman in the hat looked up, as if she had heard his thoughts, and he caught a glimpse of a snub nose, bee-stung lips and Arctic blue eyes several shades lighter than his. It was only a glimpse, but the pull between them was so instant, so intense, that he was already moving across the concourse before he remembered that he didn't know her.

His feet slowed.

Throughout his adult life, he'd grown used to being the object of a universally admiring female gaze, but this woman was staring past him. No, make that *through* him—almost as if he wasn't there, he thought, with a beat of disbelief.

As if to prove his point, she smiled coolly at one of the uniformed porters who had come scampering over to help her and then, without so much as blinking, she was sashaying past him, following her teetering trolley of luggage towards the exit.

He watched in silence. *She was quite something.* A real ice maiden. His stomach tensed with a momentary pang of regret that she was leaving.

It wasn't just those legs.

After the party, he had planned to spend his days pitting himself against the snow-covered curves of the Alps. But he would have been happy to spend a night or two exploring other softer, warmer curves. The fact that he might have had to apply a little extra heat to melt the ice first would simply have added to the challenge.

Only it was not to be and, flipping the collar of his jacket up around his neck, he walked through the sliding doors, squinting through his sunglasses at the limousines waiting patiently like a pack of dogs in the bright Alpine sunshine.

He spotted the discreet Haensli logo on the nearest car, and without removing his sunglasses greeted the uniformed chauffeur with a lazy upward flick of his head. '*Grüezi.* They're bringing the luggage. Shouldn't be long. *Tschuldigung*—'

He broke off, frowning, as his phone rang in his jacket. Fishing it out, he answered it without thinking.

'Louis?'

He swore under his breath. For the last few months— pretty much ever since his father had died and he'd gone on the mother of all benders—he'd stopped taking his CMO's calls, so the surprise in Nick's voice was more than justified.

But it was overshadowed by his own rush of irritation at being distracted enough to pick up. 'Nick…how can I help you?'

'Good morning—or should I say, *guete morge*?'

Louis winced. He didn't know what was worse. Nick's appalling Swiss German accent or the faux bonhomie in his voice.

'Something like that. Look, Nick, I've only just landed and there was turbulence on the flight,' he lied. 'I didn't get much sleep, so can we do this later or is it something urgent?'

'I don't know, Louis. You tell me.'

'What does that mean?'

He didn't bother hiding the exasperation in his voice and he heard Nick take a breath. He could almost picture his square-jawed CMO bracing his shoulders.

'You know what it means. I've been jumping through hoops these last few months, cleaning up the messes you leave behind.'

'So don't. That's what Housekeeping is for,' he said curtly.

'I'm not talking about an unmade bed or two, Louis.' Nick's voice was vibrating with barely contained frustration. 'I'm talking about your behaviour and how it impacts the brand.'

His hand tightening around the phone, Louis rolled his eyes. 'Yes, you are, but I fail to see why,' he said, with the chilling disdain he'd inherited along with his title. 'Callière is my business. I am the brand, and my behaviour is nobody's concern. But if you're worried, I don't have to go to the Haensli party.'

He knew it wouldn't come to that. As he'd just said, *he* was the brand. Without him, Callière would be just another upmarket jewellery business.

'That won't be necessary,' Nick said pacifyingly, as Louis had known he would. 'We want you to go to the party. I just need to be sure that you're going to bear in mind your responsibilities.'

Louis gritted his teeth. Could there be any word he disliked more than responsibilities? His mouth twisted. He could think of a few: relationships, love, wife—

Feeling a familiar push-me-pull-me lurch in his stomach at the mere thought of matrimony, he took a steadying breath. 'Then be sure,' he said, in the same cold tone. 'I know the score, Nick. No headlines. No scandal. No compromising photos.' *No fun*, he might have added. 'Trust me. I know what's at stake.'

He did, and Nick was overreacting.

He wasn't about to curtail his behaviour behind closed doors at the party of the year.

'Good,' Nick said quietly. 'Because I've stuck my neck a long way out for you, Louis, and I'm getting tired of trying to convince the world that your behaviour is the sign of a desperately romantic man searching for the right woman. I'll call you after the party.'

Louis stared across the heliport as his CMO's voice faded, no longer seeing the snow-covered peaks but his father's study. And just like that he was back at Waverley, facing the Duke's furious disapproval.

Fighting a queasy mix of resentment and humiliation, he hung up.

Great! So now he was supposed to be responsible for Nick's neck as well as everything else.

He swiped off his sunglasses and ran a hand over his face. Maybe he should have just stayed in Abu Dhabi.

He hated feeling like this—as if everything was being decided for him and his life wasn't his own. It made him feel desperate and trapped, so that suddenly it was hard to head off the memories. His breath caught in his throat. Normally he could keep them in the shadows. Now, though, he could feel them lining up inside his head, waiting to ambush him.

Jamming his phone back in his pocket, he nodded curtly at the chauffeur who was still waiting in front of the car, seemingly mesmerised by the ice-covered peaks.

'Let's go,' he snapped, turning towards the limo.

And then he froze, as if he himself had turned to ice. There was a woman sitting in the back seat of his limousine. And not just any woman.

His gaze leapfrogged swiftly over the white fur hat down to a pair of unmistakable slim denim-clad thighs.

It was the ice maiden.

So she had seen him. She'd just been playing hard to get. But she was definitely here to play.

A pulse of heat darted across his skin. This was not a situation he was unfamiliar with, and normally he wouldn't have thought twice. But now, here, was the wrong time, wrong place.

He turned towards the chauffeur. 'What is she doing in there?' he demanded.

The chauffeur's eyes darted nervously towards him. 'I don't know. I thought she was with you, Your Grace.'

'With me?'

'She said she was going to the Haensli, so I assumed—' The man broke off, not willing to say anything more…not needing to.

Louis swore under his breath. The chauffeur might not know the name of the woman sitting in his limo, but he knew his name, knew his reputation, and so he'd done the maths.

A little something for the weekend, sir?

'Is there a problem?'

The question, asked by a husky but distinctly female voice, made him jerk round and, glancing across the roof of the limo, he felt his breath catch in his throat.

The woman had got out of the car and, to answer his earlier question, she was every bit as tempting up close as he'd imagined. More so, even.

Heart hammering, he stared at her in silence, drinking in her wide apart blue eyes, her regal arching eyebrows and, as she swept the hat off her head, the mane of glossy dark hair that fell about her shoulders like some advert for shampoo.

Caught off guard by his somewhat intense response to a complete stranger, he frowned. 'Yes, there appears to have been a bit of a mix-up.'

More than a mix-up. It was the last thing he needed, to be spotted hooking up here with some random woman—particularly as he wasn't even hooking up with her.

'What kind of a mix-up?'

The confusion on her face was distinctly shaded with irritation and, aware that people were turning round and lifting up their sunglasses to look at them, he felt his own irritation spark. His voice was diamond hard as his eyes met hers.

'The kind that's easily remedied. Basically, you need to find yourself another limo. This one's taken.'

Another limo...?

Santa Somerville stared at the man standing on the other side of the car, her pulse racing, her head spinning as if she'd just finished one of her skating routines.

But it wasn't the outrageousness of his remark, or even the arrogant gleam in those distractingly blue eyes that was making her heart thump against her ribs.

It was him. This man. This stranger.

Except he wasn't quite a stranger.

She had seen him before—just now, inside the heliport. And even then he had seemed vaguely familiar.

As her gaze hovered over his stubbled jaw, then tracked down over his padded jacket to his crumpled black jeans, she felt hot suddenly. It had been so long since she'd looked at a man—*really* looked. After Nathan, she had not allowed herself to even glance. It had been too painful even just thinking about where looking had led, and where it would inevitably lead again.

Only with this man there had been no question of allowing herself to do anything. Her body had simply overridden her brain and she had felt an almost overwhelming urge—not to look but to touch.

She felt her face grow warm as she remembered the exact moment when she had first become aware of him.

Standing next to her mountain of luggage, she had been suddenly and randomly conscious of the hammering of her heart—and, even more randomly, of the pastry she was holding.

It hadn't made sense until she'd realised that one part of her brain was thinking about walking over and caressing the shadowed curve of his jaw, only her fingers were sticky...

And now she was thinking it again—not the sticky fingers part, but the wanting to touch his face.

He was so handsome that she couldn't quite believe she was awake.

Real men in real life just didn't look this good.

Since getting sponsored by Bryson's Ices she'd actually met quite a few famous actors, and to be honest most of them had disappointed in the flesh.

Only this man far from disappointed.

On the contrary, he over-delivered.

He was matinee-idol-handsome, those dazzling blue eyes perfectly offset by messy brown hair and the kind of clean, sculpted bone structure that made everyone around him look smudged.

As for his body—

Her mouth was suddenly dry. Professional ice skaters trained for around five hours a day, on and off the ice, so she was used to strong thighs and muscular shoulders. But that was just athleticism.

Whoever this man was, he had something more than muscle. He had an energy that made the air grow kinetic around him, like a static storm, and made her breathing lose its rhythm.

And that was why she'd deliberately turned away, ignoring both his intense blue gaze and the sharp ache of desire twisting her stomach.

It had been the only and the absolutely necessary response for someone like her—someone who had not just failed to deliver but had been exposed for doing so.

A familiar nausea clutched at her stomach and, pushing the memory away, she gripped the side of the door. 'On the contrary,' she said, in the clipped, cool voice that had helped earn her the nickname of Snow Queen on the skating circuit. 'You need to find *yourself* another limo. You see, this one is for guests of the Hotel Haensli.'

There was a short, pulsing silence as his eyes narrowed, and then he was moving, walking round the car and stalking towards her with such a sense of purpose that she took an unsteady step backwards.

'Yes, it is,' he said silkily as he stopped in front of her. 'And I think you'll find it was sent to meet *me*.'

She couldn't place his accent. One minute it was posh London schoolboy, the next it seemed to meander into a kind of transatlantic twang. But either way there was

Snippy! She glared at him, her hands clenching at her sides. Her skin was still prickling from that whisper of contact and she hated it that her body had responded so intensely to someone so utterly appalling.

What was wrong with her?

Had she learned nothing from what had happened with Nathan?

Her stomach knotted at the memory of how astonishingly and unforgivably stupid she'd been. But even if her taste in men apparently hadn't changed, she was different now.

Taking a quick, steadying breath, she glanced across the car. It was tempting to tell him exactly where he could stick his ride, only she wouldn't put it past this man to dump her by the roadside. Particularly if he found out she wasn't even staying at the hotel.

Her spine stiffened against the smooth leather upholstery. Merry had asked one of the drivers to pick her up as a favour, but officially the limo service was reserved for guests of the Haensli—not friends of the staff.

The last thing she wanted to do was get her best friend into trouble. Especially after everything Merry had done to make this happen—not just the ride in a limo but inviting her to stay at her chalet and even wangling her a ticket for the hotel's party…a party that had a guest list like a royal wedding.

Best of all, the hotel had its own private ice rink, so she could keep up with her training schedule.

She felt a sudden surge of anger. She had been so looking forward to this trip. It was the first real holiday she'd had in so long. Actually, it was pretty much the first real holiday she'd ever had.

Training to become a professional skater meant that there was little time for holidays or parties or any kind of fun, really. And anyway, not everyone was like Richie Rich over there.

Some people—most people, in fact—had to work hard for the things they wanted and needed. Her throat tightened as she pictured her small, shabby home. Her father and Kate had already sacrificed so much to make her dream a possibility, but at least now she had the Bryson's sponsorship.

Without it, she didn't know what she would do. At this level of competition there were just so many expenses. But she did know she wasn't going to let her family take care of her for the rest of her life.

'So you're staying at the hotel.'

It was a statement, not a question, but even so she felt her stomach clench in panic as she stared at the man sprawling languidly on the seat beside her. Had he guessed that she wasn't a guest?

Lifting her chin, she returned his gaze full-on. 'For the party.' That was true, not that she owed him the truth.

His gaze travelled over her face, level and considering, almost as if he could sense that she was not lying, but also not being completely honest.

'Then we have something in common, Ms...?' He let the silence fill the space between them as he waited for her to say her name.

'Somerville. Santa Somerville.'

Her real name was Santina. She was named after the little town in Italy where her parents had first met by chance on their way to Cortina. When she had been born in December it had been shortened to Santa. Only she wasn't about to share any of that with this stranger.

His blue eyes were intent on her face and her throat felt dry, tight, so that it was hard to swallow. And then she felt her face grow warmer as his mouth kicked up at one corner.

'Santa baby...' he sang softly, 'I really do want a yacht as it happens.' His smile widened. 'Actually, what I really want is a private jet. Do you think you could slip that under the tree for me?'

There wasn't a single version of that line that she hadn't heard before and, judging by that taunting smile, she was pretty sure Louis knew that. And yet there was something about the way he delivered it that sent a jolt of sexual electricity across her skin, so that suddenly she was struggling to speak.

Or maybe it was the slow, teasing smile that accompanied it.

Or the way his blue eyes held hers in a way that made her feel as though he was looking into her soul.

She felt her skin heat, and a small shiver wound through her body. She buried her fingers in the fur of the hat in her lap.

'I'm afraid not,' she said stiffly. 'I'm right out of private jets, Mr—'

'Albemarle. Louis Albemarle.'

She blinked.

Outside the limousine, she could see the picture-postcard-perfect Alpine village of Klosters, with its snow-covered shops and horse-drawn sleighs, but she barely glanced at it. She was too busy staring at Louis.

Where had she heard that name before?

Her breathing stalled, her brain scampering fever-
ishly through facts and faces as Louis leaned forward
and knocked on the window behind the driver.

'Just drop me over there. I'll walk up.'

The driver nodded. 'Yes, Your Grace.'

Your Grace.

Santa frowned. With most people the more time you
spent with them, the more you understood them. But
this man was making less and less sense.

'Why is he calling you that?' she asked slowly.

She felt pinpricks of heat on her skin as his glittering blue eyes locked with hers.

'Because that, Santa baby, is how you address a
duke.'

And just like that everything fell into place. Her
brain lit up like a row of lemons on a fruit machine as
a buzz of shock went through her body.

No wonder he had seemed so familiar.

Unlike Kate, her stepmother, she didn't follow the
lives of celebrities, but she would have had to live in a
cave or maybe on the moon not to have heard at least
something about this man's life.

Louis Albemarle, the Duke of Astbury, serial phi-
landerer, breaker of countless women's hearts, the no-
torious owner of Bijoux Callière and the subject of
countless splashy headlines.

Her heart began hammering against her chest.

She'd actually read a kiss-and-tell story about him
the other week, when she'd been waiting for a session with the physio. Some poor model he'd dated then
dumped, pouring her heart out.

Her spine tensed. The woman must have been out

of her mind to think she could trust a man like Louis, given that he had famously and cold-bloodedly jilted his bride at the wedding of the decade when he was just twenty. And, judging by that magazine story, his treatment of women hadn't improved over the last ten years.

'You're the Duke of Astbury.' She shook her head. 'Well, that explains a lot.'

He shifted forward in his seat and she felt a shiver run down her spine. His face had hardened, the teasing smile was gone and tension was visible in every angle of his muscular body.

'Only if you're naive or deluded enough to believe everything you read on the internet,' he said coolly.

'Not everything.'

She stared into his cold, handsome face, her insides lurching with shock and self-loathing as the limo started to slow.

Idiot.

The word ricocheted inside her head as she met his blue gaze. Remembering the way her body had wanted to sink into his, she bit into the side of her cheek.

Why was she so weak and foolish when it came to men?

It was bad enough that she was so susceptible to a handsome face and a few flirtatious remarks, but to be susceptible to this particular man?

'But you know what they say—there's no smoke without fire.'

His eyes narrowed fractionally. 'They also say innocent until proved guilty. But you clearly believe in trial by tabloid.'

'As opposed to what? Believing you?' She gave a humourless laugh. 'Why would I do that? You've already proved that you're not what you claim to be.'

His dark eyebrows snapped together. 'You know nothing about me.'

'I know that you're a duke, and that supposedly makes you a gentleman.' She gave him an icy stare. 'Only you didn't exactly behave like a gentleman earlier, did you?'

Santa felt the hairs stand up on the back of her neck as he leaned in closer.

'Would it have made any difference if I had?' His face hardened. 'You'd already made up your mind that I was a spoiled little rich boy in a man's body.' Thick dark lashes shielded the expression in his eyes, but his breathing wasn't quite steady as he spoke. 'But, just so you know, I'm as disappointed in you as you are in me.'

Her head jerked upwards and she felt her face drain of colour. 'What do you mean?'

His gaze didn't flicker.

'Just that you're one of the most beautiful women I've ever met. Your face is so expressive, and your eyes have this incredible *chatoyance*... Only all that radiance and sparkle means nothing...' he bit the words out softly '...because there's ice in your veins. In fact...' his fingers curled over the door handle '...I'm going to go and warm up outside.'

Her heart was in her throat and she felt raw inside. 'That suits me just fine,' she said hoarsely.

He smiled in a finite way. 'I'd wish you an enjoyable stay at the Haensli, Ms Somerville, but somehow I think that might be a bit beyond you.'

And then he was out of the limo and the door was

slammed shut. And she was alone on the smooth leather seat with a frown and a head full of scattered, unspoken retorts.

CHAPTER TWO

PICKING UP HER cup of coffee from the kitchen counter, Santa walked into the living area of Merry's chalet and stared out of the window at the blue-white mountains, wishing once again that her friend was there and not on a train somewhere in Europe.

Just fifteen minutes' walk from the hotel, it was a lovely, cosy little cabin, nothing like the glamorous Haensli, with its wood-panelled walls, leather sofas, opulent gold lamps and equally opulent Christmas tree.

When she'd walked into the hotel's vast reception area to pick up the key Merry had left for her, her legs had been shaking, her hands too. Only she hadn't been able to blame the opulent *hygge* interior. Or the nonchalant, cosmopolitan hotel patrons in their sleek down jackets, cashmere jumpers and shearling-lined boots.

'There's ice in your veins.'

Her lips formed a moue of annoyance.

No, the blame for her nervousness lay solidly at the feet of the Duke of Astbury. It had been his barbed words, so casually tossed at her just as he got out of the limo, that had made her stomach knot with a familiar panic. And those same words were still echoing inside her head now.

But why?

Fingers tightening around the cup, she shivered.

Louis didn't know her. He didn't know what had happened with Nathan.

She'd never told anyone. Not even her best friend. Merry had already left to go to college by then, and it had seemed ridiculous to dredge it up when she'd finally come home to visit.

A knot tightened in her chest. Plus, she'd been ashamed—and scared. Scared to look into her friend's eyes and see not just affection and concern but an acknowledgement that Nathan was right.

She bit her lip. So she hadn't said anything, and probably she wouldn't say anything about Louis either.

And not just because of what he'd said.

Her pulse missed a beat and another shiver skimmed over her skin, this one hot, not cool. There had been that other thing too…that tension between them in the limo.

She gritted her teeth, trying to give it a name. She wanted to call it hate, but hate was so unequivocal. It had been more like a battle of wills—a kind of virtual tug of war, with neither of them willing to let go of the rope.

It was like nothing she had ever felt before. But then Louis Albemarle wasn't like any other man she'd met.

He was a stranger, and yet he didn't feel like one. And, more confusingly, even though she disliked him intensely, she had never felt so attracted to a man. It was both baffling and irresistible. Maybe that was why it had made her feel so out of control and inadequate. Just like before. Just like with Nathan.

Her throat tightened at the memory.

She'd been so naive back then. So trusting and hopeful and eager. *And stupid.* What other explanation could there be for how she'd acted? What she'd accepted?

But it wasn't going to happen again. Particularly not with a man like Louis. She didn't want or need that kind of complication in her life—and besides there was no room.

No, what she needed was to skate.

Unzipping the sleek bag that had cost more than her plane ticket, she pulled out her skates, her fingers pressing into the smooth white leather.

Skating was her passion, but it was also the matrix of her life. Everything fitted in around it and had done so ever since she was three years old. She wasn't academic like her father, or artistic like Kate, nor was she outgoing like Merry. Skating was what she did. It made her feel confident and sure of herself.

She had wanted to go onto the rink earlier, but by the time she'd picked up the keys and unpacked and had lunch it had been too late. The rink would have been too crowded.

With that many people there was too great a danger of someone banging into her, and she couldn't risk getting injured. Not with the International Figure Skating Championships just under two years away.

She had come twelfth in the last competition and, given her age, realistically this would be her last chance for a medal. She wasn't going to do anything to jeopardise that.

Her mouth thinned. And that included getting all hot and quivery about somebody as vile and up himself as Louis Albemarle…

Without Merry's company, Santa had thought she might be at a loose end. But her days had fallen effortlessly into a pattern of mooching around the shops, drinking *kaffee-creme* at one of the town's many small restaurants, and of course skating. And she was surprised to find that she was enjoying her own company—enjoying herself full-stop.

So much for that being beyond her, she thought coolly, remembering Louis's parting shot in the limo. Not that she had seen him since that tense encounter. And she had no wish to do so, she thought, bending her knee and pushing off onto the ice.

It was the first time she'd had the rink entirely to herself and, gazing up at the blue sky and the glittering peaks, she felt a rush of exhilaration. She loved competing, but there was something special about skating here, surrounded by the majesty and untamed beauty of the mountains.

She could feel her body growing weightless, her mind emptying of everything and, moving forward, she gave herself up to the ice and the rush of crystalline air.

Weaving his way through the café, Louis scowled up at the pristine blue sky, cursing Nick under his breath.

Despite having said he would call after the party, for some reason his CMO had rung him at midnight last night. Make that midnight in Toronto. It had actually been six o'clock in the morning here.

Six.

In the morning.

Nick had left a message apologising, claiming it was a 'handbag call', but it hadn't been. Louis scowled. His CMO had been checking up on him.

Pushing back his beanie, he dropped into one of the café chairs and pulled out his phone. He felt a stab of satisfaction as the screen turned black.

'*Grüezi.* Good morning, sir. How may I help you?'

Without bothering to look round at the waiter, he said tersely, '*Kaffee-creme, bitte.*'

He'd tried going back to sleep. He'd even taken a pillow and hugged it against his stomach, like he'd used to at boarding school when he'd felt hollowed out with homesickness.

His spine tensed against the back of the chair. He hadn't done that in years, and he wished now that he hadn't done it this morning.

Pulse accelerating, he leaned forward, reaching for the coffee the waiter had discreetly placed on the table. It had been fine at first, but then, at some unspecified point, the soft, down-filled pillow had inexplicably turned into the soft curves of Santa Somerville.

Sucking in a sharp breath, he stared moodily across the ice rink to the panorama of mountains.

He wasn't crazy. He had known it wasn't her. And yet with his eyes closed and warmth spreading through his body it had been easy to pretend, to press closer—

His lip curled. Maybe if it had been a one-off, he might have ignored it, but Santa had been popping into his head at annoyingly frequent intervals throughout the last few days. More annoyingly still, he kept seeing her everywhere.

Sashaying towards the lift.

Turning away so that her shimmering dark hair swung like a cape around her shoulders.

Lowering her head over a menu in the restaurant.

Except it wasn't her.

It was just his mind playing tricks on him. Only he couldn't remember this ever happening before…this being so *fascinated* by a woman that he actually conjured her up from nothing. He gritted his teeth. Not for a long time, anyway. Not since Marina.

But at least that had made sense. He had known Marina since childhood, dated her for a year. Their families even shared some ancestors.

Santa made no sense. There had been a total of only about thirty minutes from the moment she had first spoken to him at the heliport to when he had climbed out of the limo.

Why, then, had he been thinking about her on and off for the last few days?

Probably because of what she'd said to him.

It had stung.

It still did. Almost as much as disdain.

He might be allergic to commitment and a magnet for trouble, but that didn't seem to put most women off. On the contrary, it usually made them even more eager to make his acquaintance.

He felt his body respond to the memory of just how eager. And that was fine by him. He wanted women to beg him for sex, and they did.

All except Santa Somerville.

And maybe that went a long way to explaining why she kept popping into his head. The fact that she was neither begging nor likely to beg any time soon.

A muscle pulled in his jaw. Not that she hadn't wanted to.

He knew enough about women to read the signs, and while Santa might have spent the entire limo ride hurling insults at him, her eyes had said something entirely different. He had seen the flicker of curiosity, the flare of heat there that had had nothing to do with fighting and everything to do with damp skin and tangled sheets.

Picturing her face in the limo, lips parted, eyes wide, the blue irises vivid against her flushed cheeks, he felt his groin harden.

She had wanted him as much as he'd wanted her, and if she'd been any other woman they would have retired discreetly to her room and stayed in bed until they'd been too exhausted to argue.

Instead, she'd had to turn everything into some kind of battle of wills.

Shoulders tensing against the ache of frustration in his groin, he let his narrowed gaze follow the progress of the skater out on the rink.

She was dressed in black sweatpants, a black beanie, a short hot-pink fur-trimmed jacket and white boots. He watched, mesmerised, as she performed a faultless triple axel followed by a double toe loop. He loved the rush and rhythm of skiing and snowboarding, and excelled at both, but skating had always seemed too much like hard work.

Only this skater made it look effortless, organic, like a snowflake spinning on a breeze.

He leaned forward.

She was breathtakingly good.

There were usually one or two skaters on any rink who caught the eye, and this girl had all the jumps and spins. But she had more than just technical skill. There was an emotional quality to the way she moved, an uninhibited rapture in her body's flexibility and power and grace.

She knew how to skate.

And he wasn't the only one who thought so.

Glancing round, he saw that there were quite a few people watching her now. Some were even holding up their phones, and as the skater finished up with a one-foot spin there was a smattering of applause.

He watched her skate towards the café and then, as she stepped off the ice, she pulled off the beanie and he swore softly as he saw who she was.

But of course it would have to be Santa, he thought, his gaze tracking down her legs as it had tracked her progress around the rink. He'd just been too caught up in the way she'd moved on the ice to really register her separate body parts.

Now that he had, he made up for lost time by letting his eyes linger on her toned thighs. It took approximately three seconds for him to picture them wrapped around his waist, and then he dragged his gaze up to her face.

He felt something warm and silvery snake across his skin. Her chin was jutting out combatively and instantly he sat up, his earlier lethargy vanishing like Alpine mist.

'What are you doing here?' Santa was looking at him coldly, her surprise distinctly stippled with irritation.

'I'm enjoying the view.' Raising an eyebrow provocatively, he gestured past the curve of her bottom to the mountains. 'I'm also enjoying this coffee. In fact, why don't you join me?'

Before she could reply, he glanced at one of the waiters and held up one finger, relishing the cool anger in her eyes almost as much as the curve of her bottom.

'I don't think that's a good idea,' she said crisply.

'Why? Are you worried you might give in to temptation?'

Her eyes locked with his. 'Only the temptation of thumping you.'

The coffee arrived, and he watched the play of emotions on her face as the desire to tell him where he could shove it waged war with natural good manners. Of course good manners won and, not bothering to hide his amusement, he watched her sit down, tucking her legs primly under the table.

Pulling out her phone, she glanced at the screen. 'I have ten minutes. And this is just a coffee,' she said icily.

Was it?

Looking up at her through thick, dark lashes, he saw that same flicker of heat in her gaze as he had on the limo ride—a heat that had nothing to do with irritation.

'Absolutely,' he agreed. 'There will be no pastry consumption.'

As she rolled her eyes he glanced down at her skates. They were not new, but they were expensive. Custom-made, probably. He gently pushed the one nearest to him with the toe of his boot.

'Nice skates.'

She jerked her foot away.

'Do you mind?'

'Not if you don't.'

There was something about this woman that made him want to get a rise out of her, and she was so delightfully easy to provoke, he thought, watching her cheeks flood with colour.

'I knew this was a mistake.' She started to get up, and he hooked his foot around the leg of her chair to stop her.

'Okay, okay…' He held up his hands. 'I'm sorry. I was just teasing. Please. Stay. If not for me then for Herr Frisch. If you leave he'll think that you don't like his coffee, and he'll be so upset it could set back his recovery.'

'Fine,' she snapped, sitting back in her seat. 'But move your foot.'

He stared at her in silence. How did she do it? How could she be so uptight, so stubborn, so haughty, so maddeningly infuriating, and yet still make him feel this hard and hot and hungry?

Shifting in his seat, needing to recalibrate the balance of power, he put his feet up on the chair beside her and met her gaze.

'So how long have you been skating?'

She hesitated, her expression still frosty. 'Since I was three.'

'Well, that explains a lot.' He'd picked his words carefully, wondering if she would remember saying exactly the same sentence to him in the limo. Watching her glacier-blue eyes narrow, he knew she had.

'Meaning?'

Meaning that it was no surprise. Because she was so at one with herself when she skated. She was an ice princess, and the rink was her realm, he thought, his gaze taking in her shining dark hair and the flush of colour on her amazing cheekbones.

Glancing down at her clenched hands, he sat forward, reaching for his coffee. Probably best not to say that. The last thing he needed was to turn up at the party tomorrow with a black eye.

'You seem at home on the ice. Let me guess… Your parents skate?'

'My mother.' Her voice was as cool as the clear mountain air, but something in the tilt of her head made his pulse accelerate.

'And did you inherit your looks from her as well as your talent?'

Giving him a withering look, she jerked the chair beside her backwards, so that his feet fell to the floor.

'I don't know. Did you inherit your arrogance and general air of entitlement when you became a duke?'

Wow, he thought. She might look like a porcelain doll, but she punched low and hard.

'Unfortunately not,' he said softly, hooking the chair and drawing it closer again, to put his feet back up on it. 'My father only died three months ago, but I've always been this arrogant and entitled.'

Her lip curled and she tutted under her breath. That amazed him. He didn't know anyone who still tutted their disapproval. Most people these days just swore routinely.

'Is that why you chose the Haensli? Because of the rink?'

She glanced away, a flush of colour creeping over her cheeks. 'Not particularly. But it's a bonus. I like to skate every day.'

He watched as she leaned forward and began tugging at the laces.

'Every day? That's a serious hobby.'

'Well, you know me.' Sliding her feet into hiking boots, she raised perfectly groomed eyebrows. 'Fun doesn't play a major part in my life.'

He stared at her in silence. His remark had clearly got under her skin, and the trickle of excitement that had started when he was watching her skate surged. Actually, he didn't know her—but he wanted to.

Or at least he wanted to know what lay beneath that padded jacket and how he could make her body arch like it had out on the ice.

'But skating does?' he said.

Her hair was tied up today, and as she nodded her ponytail swung in time to the movement of her head. There was a pause, and he could almost see her calibrating her thoughts, choosing what to give away, what to conceal.

Finally, she sighed. 'I'm a figure skater.'

Now that he knew, it made perfect sense: the poise, the sense of purpose.

And the mother.

Not many three-year-olds were articulate enough to demand skating lessons, and in his experience talented sportsmen and women usually had supportive parents behind them. The kind of parents who put their own lives on hold to encourage their children.

His chest tightened.

Not that he would know anything about that personally. After he'd stood Marina up at the altar his parents had not only failed to support him, they had banished him from their lives—privately, anyway.

Even though they knew the truth.

Even though he was their son, their only child.

He felt it inside—that familiar rush of rage and resentment and hurt…a hurt he didn't usually allow himself to feel. But it was hard to ignore it when he met someone like Santa—someone who had two parents who actually loved her.

'So that was a routine?' Blanking his mind, he gestured towards the rink.

She hesitated again, and he stared at her mouth, watching her bite into the soft cushion of her lower lip.

'It was part of a routine.'

He frowned. 'Don't you need music for that?'

'Usually. But I can't wear headphones when there could be other skaters on the ice. It would be dangerous.' Her slim fingers smoothed out a crease in the napkin that had come with her coffee and he felt a pulse of heat beat across his skin. It was all too easy to picture those same fingers moving smoothly over his body.

'So what do you do instead?'

She looked startled, her forehead creasing as if his question had surprised her, and he fought the urge to lean over and smooth away the furrows.

'I don't do anything. I just skate,' she said simply.

He stared at her, envying both the light in her winter ice eyes and the tightness of her focus. Everything about her was the opposite of how he felt about himself. His life seemed so aimless, so reactive. So curtailed...

Taking a breath to ease the sudden tightness in his throat, he shook his head. 'No, that wasn't "just" skating. Skating is a discipline. You have to learn how to move on the ice. What you did out there...how you moved... No one could learn that. It was unthinking. Like water flowing—'

She blinked. 'What?'

With her legs concealed beneath the table, and her body hidden under that quilted jacket, it should have been easier for him to think clearly, but apparently not. And as her gaze sharpened on his face he shifted back in his seat, his gut knotting, feeling suddenly on edge and exposed in a way that he hadn't allowed to happen for years.

Like water flowing. Where the hell had that come from? More importantly, what on earth had possessed him to say it out loud?

The café was filling up now and, looking across the tables, he noticed a group of young women staring over at him appreciatively.

He felt his pulse jump. Women like that—women with endless smiles and short attention spans—were reassuringly straightforward. There was none of this frustrating getting the wrong end of the stick, like with the woman sitting opposite him.

Eyes narrowing, he met their collective gaze, his

smile automatic, unfiltered, inclusive, and then, still smiling, he returned his attention to Santa. 'What I'm trying to say is that you're good. Very good. Seriously. You have a real talent.'

That was better. It was true, but it was also the kind of generic remark anyone might make.

Only he knew as soon as he'd spoken that he'd said something wrong.

She tensed, her face not so much hardening as turning to stone. 'You don't need to say that.'

His lazy smile felt suddenly stupid and inappropriate, like a clown's bowtie at a funeral, and he felt his own face tense too. 'I know I don't.'

'No, I mean you don't have to tell me that just because you want to go to bed with me.'

'That's not why I said it.' He felt a flash of rage as she gave him one of those snooty little looks she seemed to specialise in.

'Of course it wasn't,' she said tartly, her eyes narrowing, one small boot tapping impatiently on the floor. 'I don't know which is more ludicrous. Your thinking we might sleep together, or the idea that I would actually fall for your half-hearted attempt to flatter me into doing so.'

Now his temper didn't so much fray as rip in two.

'Okay—just so we're clear—I don't need to use tricks or flattery to get women into my bed. Believe me, baby, most times I don't even have to open my mouth.'

She was staring at him as if he had suddenly grown scales. 'If only this moment was one of those times.'

Anger rolling through him like an avalanche, Louis

watched Santa reach into her pocket and pull out a cluster of notes.

'You know, just for a moment there I thought you were almost nice.'

'Yeah, well, just for a moment I thought you were almost human,' he snarled. 'But I was wrong. You really do have ice in your veins.'

'And you have a one-track mind, Your Grace.' Snatching up her skates, she rose from her chair like a queen from her throne. 'But you'll have to find someone else to be one of your pitstops on this particular journey, because I'm not interested.' She glanced pointedly at the group of giggling women. 'Enjoy the view.'

Louis stared after her, fury and disbelief pounding in his veins. That was the second time she'd given him the cold shoulder—metaphorically and literally—and the second time she had blamed him for something he hadn't done.

Well, now he was done with her.

Done with her strange swerves of mood and her willingness to judge him.

She thought she was all that, with her glossy dark hair and those mouthwatering legs. But even if his life had been his own, and Nick hadn't been keeping him on such a short leash, he wouldn't have remotely considered hooking up with a woman like Santa. Why would he? She wasn't even his type. She was too tense. Too serious. And no fun. He was just bored, and frustrated, and looking to be distracted.

A slow, curling smile tugged at the corners of his mouth.

Fortunately, it just so happened that the perfect distraction would be taking place right here, tomorrow evening. After all, how long could it possibly take for a party chock-full of beautiful women to erase the memory of Santa Somerville?

Heart thumping, Santa made her way through the café and into the street. Panic was rising in her head like neat alcohol.

She was shocked by how close she had got to letting down her guard with Louis. A few questions here…a smile there. Was that all it took for her to forget everything she knew about him? Everything she knew about herself?

She left both those questions unanswered as she walked swiftly up the street to Merry's chalet.

Her heart was pounding like a drum and she felt unbearably conscious of her inadequacy as a human—as a woman.

Probably Louis had just been spinning her a line, but what had scared her was the thought that he wasn't. That he might have meant what he said. Because then she would have to make a choice.

Only there was no choice—not really. She wasn't that brave. But it hurt so much to admit that, and as she pushed the key in the lock she wished suddenly that Merry was there to make her laugh—

The door opened.

'There you are. I was just coming to look for you.' Glancing down at the skates in Santa's hand, Merry rolled her eyes. 'I knew you wouldn't be able to help yourself. Honestly, this is supposed to be a holiday.'

Santa blinked back her tears and hurled herself into her friend's arms. 'It is now.'

Walking into the Hotel Haensli felt very different this time round, Santa thought, carefully lifting the hem of her skirt so that she didn't tread on it.

For starters, Merry was here. *Merry.* Her friend—her best friend—the one person outside of her family who had always looked out for her and looked after her.

It also helped that they were using the staff entrance.

'Are you okay?'

Merry was looking at her anxiously.

Injecting a bright note into her voice, she nodded. 'I'm fine. Truly. And I'm going to have fun tonight. I promise.'

Smiling, she gave Merry's hand a reassuring squeeze. She knew why her friend was worried about her. As a child she'd been paralyzingly shy. She still was inside, and she didn't have—would never have—Merry's confidence. Fortunately, skating competitively had forced her to meet so many strangers that at least now she could string two words together.

She still wasn't good at big events, but just for once Merry didn't need to be worrying about her—particularly as her friend didn't seem to be her usual serene self. In fact, after their initial joy at seeing one another had faded, for the first time in their lives they had struggled to keep the conversation going.

Probably, she told herself sternly, because Merry was tired after her trip and had a lot more on her mind than Santa. Like helping to organise the biggest, most glamorous party in Europe.

She slipped in her shoes and almost lost her balance, and Merry giggled. It was a running joke between them that Santa moved like a swan out on the ice but a duck on dry land, particularly in heels. But it wasn't just her heels that were making her feel unsteady. There was every chance she was going to see Louis tonight, and she would be lying if she claimed that thought didn't agitate and unnerve her.

Not that Merry could know that.

As predicted, she hadn't told her anything about Louis other than that they'd shared a limo and he had been unbelievably arrogant, and she felt a flicker of guilt at not confiding in her friend. Only she couldn't even begin to think how to lead into that particular conversation. And she didn't have to. Not here and now anyway.

'Will we do?'

Merry was smiling at her. She had borrowed a dress, but it looked as if it had been made for her. She looked beautiful, her pale pink gown offsetting her delicate beauty perfectly.

Santa pretended to consider. 'I think so.'

They were still giggling as they reached the doors of the ballroom. As they embraced one another tightly, Santa swallowed. Her throat was dry and tight, and her hands felt shaky.

As if sensing her nerves, Merry whispered, 'You don't have to hide in the shadows—or in the bathroom! Stay with me as much as you want.'

But that wasn't going to happen. Not tonight.

Santa shook her head and forced her smile to widen. 'Don't you worry about me. Just go to work before you get into trouble.'

Smile stiffening, she watched Merry scamper away through the throng of guests. Taking a deep breath, she smoothed her dress with a slightly unsteady hand. She had made Merry a promise and she was going to keep it.

Tonight she was going to have fun. She was going to enjoy herself. In fact, she was going to be so busy enjoying herself that she wouldn't even notice if Louis Albemarle was at the party or not.

CHAPTER THREE

SANTA STARED DAZEDLY around the Haensli's ballroom. It looked like something out of a children's picture book— a fairy tale winter wonderland, complete with snow-flecked Christmas trees and a backdrop of spinning snowflakes that looked as if they were made of real diamonds.

Even without the stunning decor it was a beautiful room, high-ceilinged and with huge windows along the length of one side that offered a world-class view of the mountains. It was the perfect setting for the per-fect Christmas party.

And she felt like a fraud…an imposter.

Despite her promise to Merry, since her friend had scampered off to work Santa had hardly spoken a word to anyone, and in desperation she took a sip of her cock-tail, hoping it might shift the knot of nervous apprehen-sion in her diaphragm.

It ought to. The Figgy Fizz was a delicious festive mix of vodka, Cointreau, plum liqueur and Prosecco, garnished with edible gold spray.

It was also very potent.

She took another cautious sip. Her training schedule

more or less made drinking impossible, so she wasn't used to alcohol. Not that she would ever drink much anyway. Growing up, she'd listened to everyone talking about 'getting hammered' and sometimes had thought about doing it. It would certainly have made it easier to fit in.

But she'd always been too scared of the consequences.

How could she get drunk after what had happened to her mother?

She couldn't have looked herself in the eye, much less her father.

Only surely tonight was an exception?

She was on holiday, and Merry was here somewhere. What harm could there be in having a bit of fun? Or even a lot? In fact, now she thought about it, she was absolutely committed to having a whole lot of fun tonight.

She'd show the Duke of Astbury just how wrong he'd been…

She sucked in a breath, a flicker of irritation snaking up inside her. What was he doing in her head?

Back in her head, she should say.

Since she'd left the café yesterday Louis had appeared with frustrating regularity in her thoughts.

Not just his words. Everything about him. Like the way it had seemed the entire café had surreptitiously and collectively focused its attention on him as he'd nudged her foot with his toe…the way he'd brushed his thumb against the rim of his coffee cup…and of course his face—that absurdly handsome face.

How was anyone supposed to *not* think about that face?

She swallowed hard, her throat suddenly dry. After

today's session on the ice she was going to have to try. It had been the worst she'd ever skated. She had kept losing focus, making stupid mistakes, and stumbling more than once.

Even now, most of her nervousness was down to the thought of bumping into Louis. As if to prove her point, she felt her eyes dart across the room, involuntarily seeking one particular dark head among the sea of other heads.

But she wasn't going to let this strange, errant attraction get in the way of her goal. She was stronger than that. She would do whatever it took to get him out of her head for good.

And she didn't really have to worry about seeing him at this party. Men like Louis Albemarle were late for everything and women like her always left early, so their paths wouldn't overlap.

She felt her insides tighten as a group of men in immaculate evening dress and women swathed in sequins and satin greeted one another with a flurry of air kisses and, 'Where did you get that dress, darling? You look amazing!'

She felt as if everyone knew each other except her.

But, really, what difference would it make even if she knew every single person here? Look at school. Most of the other students had ignored her, a couple had tolerated her and a loud-mouthed few had pointedly disliked her. Her social life had been limited to a handful of parties, where she'd spent most of her time hiding in the bathroom.

Merry had told her that they were all jealous because she had everything they wanted. Looks, brains, talent… But at school she had been small and skinny, with a brace—she still wore a retainer some nights. As for brains… She had been okay at some subjects, but she certainly hadn't been top of the class. And most of her classmates had never even seen her skate. All they'd known about her 'talent' was that she got to have days off school for competitions.

Merry was just being a good friend, as usual.

Her hand felt cold against the glass and she stared around the room, wishing suddenly that Merry was there with her. But she was a big girl now, and Merry was working. She couldn't expect her to be her baby-sitter all night.

Taking another sip of her cocktail, she edged away from the excited throng of guests and made her way to the tall windows.

If only she could somehow transfer the poise she found on the ice into real life. Out there, she didn't need alcohol to feel confident. When she skated, she felt powerful and strong and free.

Her heartbeat stalled.

She didn't know how, but Louis had been right about that. It *did* feel as if she was flowing…the stretch of her muscles was unthinking. It was something over which she had no conscious choice, like breathing. It wasn't snarled up with fear of fitting in or saying the wrong thing.

'Excuse me?'

It was an American voice, female.

She spun round, her eyes widening, to find two young women, one blonde and one brunette, staring at her as if they had stumbled across a unicorn.

The blonde, who was wearing a low-cut white dress that oozed over her body without a ripple, bit into the smile curving her scarlet lips. 'You're that skater, aren't you? Santa Somerville.'

Santa felt her face grow warm. She didn't often get recognised away from the rink.

Figure skating was only really on most people's radar during the big, televised competitions, and even then, not everyone connected the make-up-free young woman in casual clothing with the poised skater in her competition costumes with her hair pulled back into a bun.

But tonight, courtesy of Merry's nimble fingers, her hair was in some kind of complicated twisted updo, and as well as wearing mascara and smoky eyeshadow she had painted her lips the colour of ripe berries to match her dress.

'Yes, I am.' She smiled stiffly.

'I knew it,' the brunette said triumphantly. 'I saw you skating yesterday at the rink and I thought I recognised you. You are amazing. I totally loved your last routine.'

Santa smiled. 'Thank you. I wish you'd been one of the judges.'

'Honestly, you're an incredible skater. I look like Bambi when I skate—you know, with my legs going in opposite directions.' As Santa laughed, the brunette waggled her drink. 'The only kind of ice I'm comfortable with comes in a glass.'

'Yeah, you should have one of these.' The blonde held up her own glass. 'It's called an Iceberg. Pastis and vodka. It's absolutely lethal. I'm Lauren, by the way.' Giggling, she clinked glasses with the brunette. 'And this is Chloe.'

'I love your dress.' Chloe sighed. 'You have such great legs.'

'Thank you.' Smiling, and desperate to think of something to say, Santa said quickly, 'I love your bracelets.' Both women were wearing identical bands studded with diamonds around their wrists.

Lauren giggled. 'We gave them to each other last Christmas. We have earrings to match, but we're not wearing them tonight.' She lowered her voice. 'You know the goodie bags they give you when you leave? Apparently Callière is giving away diamond earrings.'

Chloe fanned her face. 'I'd rather have the Duke of Astbury in my goodie bag. He is so hot—and he really knows how to party.'

Santa felt her pulse thud inside her head. It was the first time she had heard his name spoken out loud and her body froze. She felt suddenly like a hunted animal at the thought that he might be somewhere here in the huge ballroom.

Resisting the urge to glance round and check, she smiled as Lauren nodded. 'I know he's wild, but who doesn't love a bad boy?'

Me, Santa thought. *I don't.* What was there to love? Louis was rude and arrogant and spoiled and selfish. And beautiful, and sexier than any man had a right to be, her brain unhelpfully finished.

As both women made enthusiastic noises Santa kept her smile pasted to her face, but their reaction had sent a burn of jealousy through her body.

Only why?

She might be able to admit that Louis was stupidly handsome—privately, at least—but she didn't want him in her life, much less her bed. And yet for some incomprehensible reason it hurt to think of him with another woman.

'Speaking of which…' Catching her eye, Chloe winked. 'There's a private party in one of the suites, and we were thinking we might go and hang out upstairs until it kicks off down here. You should come with us.'

Santa stared at her mutely, her pulse beating out of time. At school and college she'd always been at the bottom of the ladder when it came to the social hierarchy, and she knew that her feeling of exhilaration at this invitation merely proved how uncool she was. But she couldn't stop the warm rush of pleasure from unfurling inside her at being neither an observer nor an intruder.

Oh no—

Her whole body tensed.

The noise in the ballroom was swelling, like an orchestra warming up. But somehow, through all the chatter, she heard quite distinctly the high, purring laughter of not one but several women. More specifically, the blissed-out purr of women who had just opened their stockings on Christmas morning to find not just the deeds to a diamond mine but the mine's owner.

She gritted her teeth.

There was only one man who could cause such a stir among members of her sex.

Her heart lurched. She could practically see Louis, his taunting blue eyes drifting over the women in their brightly coloured dresses, enjoying the view. No doubt he was planning on taking a closer look later on. Not that she cared. They were welcome to him.

But as she turned her head she caught a glimpse of brown hair, and just like that her bravado drained away.

Downing her drink, she snatched another from a passing waiter and turned to Chloe, smiling brightly. 'I'd love that. Shall I follow you?'

By the time they reached the lift her glass was already half empty and the alcohol was rising to her head in a rush. But now that they had left the ballroom, and the chances of bumping into Louis were fading, she felt calmer again—and a little bit euphoric. She had never been invited to a private party before. Or at least not one that wasn't either a family event or part of her job as a Bryson's Ices ambassador.

She felt a tiny prickle of guilt that she was leaving the ballroom. Merry had gone to so much trouble to get her a ticket. But she knew her friend would understand. And it would only be for a short time. Maybe she would take a selfie to show her, she thought, as the lift arrived and Lauren grabbed her hand and dragged her inside.

She barely registered what floor they were on as the lift stopped and the doors opened. Her head was spinning, and she was too busy trying to make sense of what Lauren and Chloe were saying.

As they stopped in front of a door it opened abruptly, flooding the hallway with a pounding bassline and a buzz of conversation as a tall blond man with a sharp, pale face swayed towards them.

Chloe gave a scream. 'Oh, my goodness, Sebastian! I didn't know you were here.'

Everyone except Santa screamed too.

'She used to date Sebastian back in the day. They were at Beau Soleil together,' Lauren said loudly in her ear as they made their way through a throng of people into the room. 'His father's a prince of somewhere with a really long name that I can't pronounce.'

Santa nodded wordlessly, but she wasn't really listening.

So this was how the other half lived.

She gazed across the room, her heart hammering hard. It was a microworld of enviable luxury. Pale grey walls, an immense fireplace with an actual fire, and a deep private balcony with breathtaking views of the snow-covered peaks outside.

Not that anyone was looking at the view.

Her eyes darted to the dark green velvet sofas where not one but three famous film stars were deep in conversation. Everyone was too busy being seen to notice anyone else.

Not everyone.

Suddenly aware that she was being watched, she turned, and her breath caught in her throat, her blood freezing.

Louis was standing about ten feet away, an empty glass hanging loosely from his fingers. Like every other man there he was dressed in black tie, but he still hugged all the attention, thanks to his stunningly handsome face.

A face that was currently as still as the mountains outside and about as friendly.

As his eyes locked with hers she felt a shiver of ice and fire flicker over her skin, and her heartbeat tripped over itself like it did when she popped her jumps out on the ice. Her head was spinning again…only this time it was with panic, not alcohol.

For a moment his being there made no sense. He was downstairs in the ballroom...

Except that he clearly wasn't. And just as clearly she suddenly knew that if anyone was going to be at some exclusive private party then it would be Louis.

She swore silently. Why had she drunk those cocktails so fast? Why had she drunk them at all? Louis was the last man she wanted to see, particularly when he was dressed like that.

She stole a glance across the room, her gaze taking in the hard, high cheekbones, the straight, aristocratic nose and teasing mouth. It hurt to look at him. More than that, there was something about him that made her feel unsteady, vulnerable, out of control. And she knew that it was a feeling that had everything to do with bodies and skin and heat.

In other words: sex.

Move, she told herself as he started to weave between the guests towards her. But her legs felt as if they had frozen solid, and she could only stand and stare as he stopped in front of her.

Hoping that her face didn't look as hot as it felt, she glared at him. 'I can't say I'm surprised to see you here.'

'I should hope not,' he drawled. 'I, however, am a little surprised to see you. But perhaps not as surprised as your sponsor would be.' His gaze dropped to the empty cocktail glass in her hand and he smiled mockingly. 'Are you drunk, Santa baby?'

Was she what?

Santa stared at him in outrage. 'Don't call me that,' she snapped, fighting an impulse to slap his handsome face. Ignoring her accelerating pulse, she angled her chin up to meet his gaze. 'What I am is none of your concern, Your Grace. Now, if you don't mind, I'm going to find my friends. Oh, and please don't feel that you have to come over and talk to me again. I really won't be the least bit offended if you don't.'

She had intended to march past him with her head held high, but he stepped sideways and blocked her, his blue eyes locking with hers.

'If you were a man, I'd ask you to step outside for talking to me like that.'

Her heart felt as if it was pounding in her throat. 'If you were a man, I'd be worried. But, as we both know you're a spoiled little boy, now, let me pass or I'll call Security and have you thrown out.'

'Of my own party?'

Staring at Santa's furious face, Louis felt his entire jaw tense, but he barely registered his anger or hers. His head was still reeling from the moment when he'd looked up and seen her standing there. Unsurprisingly, given how they had parted company at the café.

His shoulders stiffened as he remembered her icy disdain. He had never been turned down with such cool, unblinking certainty. In fact, he'd never been turned down. Not to his face, anyway.

Yet here she was. In his suite. Still swatting at him with those imperious, judgemental little smiles.

Some things had changed, though. Last time they'd met she had been wrapped up against the cold. Now...

Pulse accelerating, he looked down at Santa in silence. After she'd stormed out of the café he'd been so frustrated at not having had the last word that he'd ended up looking her up on the internet.

She had started competing as a child. Despite a very promising career, for no apparent reason she had lost form a few years ago. Now, though, not only was she steadily inching her way up the rankings, with several bronze medals and a silver in her last few competitions, she'd also netted herself a sponsorship deal with Bryson's Ices. As their brand ambassador, she'd even had some ridiculous ice cream named after her: the Santa Swizzle, a sickly sounding confection involving a vanilla snow cone dipped in white chocolate with a spun sugar crown.

He wasn't surprised Bryson's Ices had picked her. They were a family brand, run by a devoted family man, and with her shy, serious smile, her wide blue eyes and enamelled cheeks Santa ticked all the boxes.

His gaze swept over Santa. What did surprise him was that dress…

It might have long sleeves and a neckline that modestly skimmed her collarbone, but it was anything but shy, he thought, unable to look anywhere except at the long length of smooth bare leg peeking out from between one of the two thigh-high slits at the front of the glossy dark purple skirt.

He felt his body stiffen, responding to the glimpse of bare skin like a dog to a stick as his gaze travelled down to her teetering red heels.

Why hadn't she just stuck to the rules? She wasn't supposed to be here, dressed like that. Hell, she wasn't supposed to be here at all.

Hardening his gaze to match his groin, he took a step

forward. 'You want to call Security? Be my guest. Except you're not, are you? My guest, I mean.' The softness in his voice in no way disguised the taunting note in his voice. 'You're just a gate crasher. Whereas I am the Duke of Astbury.'

Purple was definitely her colour, he thought, his gaze homing in on the berry-stained mouth that was currently pursing into a pout. He watched her fingers curl into fists, and then her outrage bubbled up. He caught another distracting glimpse of her legs as she took a step towards him.

'You are a horrible person.'

'So you keep saying and yet you can't keep away from me, can you?'

Her chin jutted. 'I didn't come here to see you.'

'That's right,' he mocked. 'Because you are—' raising his hands, he made quotation marks in the air '—"not interested" in me.'

'I'm not,' she snapped.

He glanced over at her flushed cheeks and saw the pulse leaping frantically against the delicate skin of her throat. He felt his body grow even harder. He wanted her and he knew she felt the same way. She just didn't want to admit it, to herself, much less to him.

'Then perhaps you need to tell that to your optic nerves.' He accompanied his words with a cynical smile. 'Because you can't take your eyes off me.'

She glared at him. 'You are impossibly arrogant.'

'And you are a hypocrite.' Still smiling, he watched a faint tremor sweep over her body as she fought for control. 'You might not like it. You might not like me. But admit it: you want me.'

Now her cheeks flamed with colour. 'In your dreams.'

Louis stared at her, a beat of heat pulsing down his spine. 'If you want it to be real, baby, you're going to have to ask.'

'What?' Her eyes widened to saucer-like dimensions and she made a noise somewhere between a gulp and a gasp.

'You heard,' he said softly.

Glancing over her shoulder, as if someone else might be listening, she shook her head. 'I'm not having this conversation with you here.'

'Fine,' he said softly, deliberately misunderstanding her. 'Let's go somewhere more private.'

He knew she would never take the bait, but he couldn't stop himself from giving the line a little tug, just to watch her squirm.

Her fingers twitched, and just for a second or two he half expected to feel her hand against his cheek, but instead she made to move past him. Only her shoe caught in the hem of her dress and she stumbled.

He reached for her automatically, his hands sliding around her waist to catch her, and he felt a sharp sting of satisfaction as her breath hitched in her throat. But there was no fear in her eyes, just fire, and he knew why she was so angry.

It was the same reason he was angry.

She felt it too—that sexual pull, that heat and hunger he couldn't remember feeling before. She was just as in thrall to it as he was, and the thought of hearing her confess her desire almost unmanned him.

'Face it, Santa, you want me. You're just too proud to admit it.'

'And *you're* just too used to getting your own way... getting what you want.' Her eyes blazed like marquise sapphires. 'But not every woman finds your charms irresistible, Louis.'

He heard the challenge in her voice, and suddenly nothing mattered more than finding some way to dent her infuriatingly lofty complacency. 'Are you sure about that, Santa?'

For a few half-seconds she stared up at him mutely, wide-eyed, her lips curling disdainfully, and then he pulled her against him with a sudden jerky movement and brought his mouth down on hers.

He felt her hands press against his shoulders and then she leaned into him, her fingers sliding down to grip his biceps. Lust punched him in the gut like a prizefighter.

Now it was his turn to almost lose his footing.

Her mouth was soft, like the softest rose petal, and his head swimming, heart pounding, blood racing, he parted her lips and deepened the kiss.

She tasted so sweet. Dark, like berries and wine. Wanting more, he wrapped one hand around her waist, the other tightening on her hip as she pulled him closer, so that he could feel her small, firm breasts pressing against the muscled wall of his chest.

Her kiss was frantic, almost clumsy, as if she was out of practice, but there was something exciting about her lack of proficiency. It felt real in a way that kissing other women didn't. The blindness of her passion, the way she was melting into him, made him feel harder and hotter than he'd ever been in his life.

His hand slid round to the dip in her back, fingers splaying possessively over the curve of her bottom.

Around them, the sounds of the party were fading. He felt the slide of her bare thigh between his legs and his stomach clenched and a savage, clamouring need jack-knifed through his body.

'Excuse me, Your Grace.'

Behind him, someone—a man—cleared his throat, and as if a spell had been broken Santa stumbled backwards out of his arms.

The noise of the party hit him like a train.

He stared dazedly down at her, shocked at the sudden and uncontrollable passion that had flared between them. Blood was roaring in his ears.

He had wanted to get under her skin. Instead, she had got under his.

Utterly disorientated, Santa stared up at Louis. Her whole body was pulsing with a hunger that was so powerful she had to struggle not to reach over and grab him by the lapels and beg him to kiss her again.

'I'm very sorry to bother you, Your Grace…' The man standing behind Louis took a tentative step forward.

'Not now, Herr Widner,' Louis snapped, without looking round.

He looked as dazed as she felt, she thought, her heart thumping against her ribs. Streaks of colour highlighted his magnificent cheekbones, and his blue eyes were blazing like a winter sunrise.

'My apologies, Your Grace.'

She watched, her thoughts scrambling for a footing, as Herr Widner gave a nervous smile and Louis finally swung round to look at him.

'But you did ask us to let you know when the security team arrived.'

Louis swore under his breath. 'And now I know. So if you wouldn't mind?'

Santa could tell that Herr Widner was forcing the smile that was stretched so determinedly across his face. 'Of course, Your Grace. But I will need your signature.'

He held out a tablet to Louis, who snatched it out of his hand.

'Fine. Where do I sign?' he snarled.

Santa breathed out shakily. Shock at what had just happened, and the part she'd played in it, was starting to chill her skin and, glancing round, she saw that quite a few of the guests were stealing surreptitious glances at her.

What was she doing? Why was she still standing here? Hadn't she made a big enough fool of herself for one night?

The memory of that night with Nathan was suddenly fresh in her head, and she was struggling to breathe. She certainly didn't need to hang around for any humiliating post-mortem, and before she even knew what she was doing she had grabbed the hem of her skirt and spun round.

She felt rather than saw Louis turn towards her, maybe even reach for her, but by then she had bolted through the nearest gap in the crowd and was skirting the perimeter of the room, moving swiftly, heading for the door.

Only she had gone the wrong way.

No, no, no—it was a bedroom.

Heart thumping, she tapped a woman in a gorgeous sequined dress on the arm. 'Sorry…is there a bathroom?'

'Just there.' The woman swayed, pointing. 'Don't be long, though,' she slurred. 'We're all heading downstairs now.'

But Santa wasn't listening.

Please let it be empty, she pleaded silently.

It was. She shut the door and locked it, her breath coming in panicky gasps. Her hands were shaking, and they felt hot and clammy. She made her way to the sink and turned on the cold tap. Staring at her reflection, she felt her heart thumping against her ribs. Her eyes were huge and dazed and her mouth looked pinkly swollen.

It was like looking at a stranger.

Lifting her hand, she touched her lower lip. She felt like a stranger too, and it wasn't just her lip that felt different. There was an unfamiliar ache deep in her pelvis…an exquisite, tingling warmth that she'd never felt before.

Turning off the tap, she dried her hands, trying to tame her heartbeat, trying to contain, to smooth away, the memory of that kiss.

Only could you smooth away something that had torn a hole in the firmament of your life?

She breathed out shakily.

It was quiet on the other side of the door now. Everyone must have gone downstairs.

And so should she.

But what if Louis was waiting for her?

A shiver of heat ran down her spine. If she saw him

again, on his own, she wasn't sure she would be able to resist him.

Maybe it would be safer to wait just a little longer.

She couldn't believe what had just happened. She should have slapped him. Or pushed him away. But she hadn't done either of those things. Instead she had melted into him like butter on a warm knife.

But it hadn't been all her fault.

How could she have known that kisses could be like that? She had only ever kissed one other man, and kissing Louis was nothing like kissing Nathan.

The touch of his mouth had stunned her. It had been a sensual exploration that had made her head swim and her body feel hot and tight with need. A need that hadn't been rational or understandable, yet had felt shockingly, devastatingly compelling.

And it wasn't as if her uncontrollable response had been private…

How many people had seen them kiss?

Her mouth trembled. None that would care. They were all rich and famous and they all knew Louis. They knew what he was like.

She did too—and that was the worst part. She knew what he was like and it hadn't made any difference to the way she'd acted because she wasn't any different. She was still that same lonely girl who wanted to be special to someone for something other than her skating.

Only here she was…still hiding in the bathroom at a party.

Her gaze jumped across the room, from the huge sunken bath to an alpaca fleece rug that covered half the floor, and then over to the voluptuous curved white sofa beside the window, with its spectacular mountain view.

It was a very palatial bathroom, but a bathroom none-theless.

She breathed out shakily. The party was over for her. She couldn't face meeting Louis again, and if Merry saw her she would know instantly that something had happened. She didn't want her friend to feel she had to worry about her tonight of all nights. No, it was time to go home.

Smoothing down her dress, she took a couple of steadying breaths and turned the door handle.

She frowned. What was wrong with it? She turned it the other way, then rattled it. But the door stayed stub-bornly shut.

'Hello? Is anyone there?' She banged on the door. 'Hello? Can anyone hear me?'

But there was no reply. Because of course everyone had gone to the party.

Biting her lip, she sat down on the sofa. She wasn't going to call Merry—she just wasn't. Maybe she could call Reception. But she didn't really want to have to explain why she was in Louis Albemarle's bathroom.

Feeling suddenly exhausted, she gazed out of the window, watching the snowflakes spiral to the ground.

There was no need to panic. She just needed to think of the best way out of this situation. Only she felt so tired. Not just tired of being locked in this bathroom, but tired of being so timid, so scared. Scared of kissing and being kissed. Scared of where kissing might lead. And most of all scared of what Louis might say after-wards. Of the look on his face...

She shivered. She hated being this person. Being someone who let fear rule them. Being so cowardly. None of this would have happened if she hadn't been scared of looking into Louis's eyes and finding Nathan staring back at her.

Careless of her hair and make-up, she lay down, pressing her face against the doe-soft Alcantara. It reminded her of her mother's coat, the one she'd always worn to the ice rink. And, feeling a little calmer, she closed her eyes, pressing her hands against the dip of her stomach where she had felt that traitorous, melting thrill.

The night seemed to go on for ever. Every half an hour or so she thought about calling someone and pulled out her phone, only for something to stop her. In the end she just lay there, watching the snow fall and at some point she must have dozed off.

She woke with a start. Outside it was still snowing, but it was no longer dark. Her heart began to pound and, pulling out her phone, she stared at the screen in dismay.

It couldn't be that time.

She couldn't have slept for that long.

Only she had.

Standing up, she almost ran across the room. She began to twist the handle, but as she did so the door abruptly opened.

'What the—'

She heard a familiar deep male voice swear, and then, looking up, met an equally familiar pair of captivating blue eyes.

There was a beat or two of silence, and then Louis said softly, 'You know, I'm sure there's a perfectly simple explanation for you being here, but please don't feel that you have to share it with me.' His eyes narrowed. 'I really won't be the least bit offended if you don't.'

CHAPTER FOUR

STARING DOWN AT SANTA, Louis gave a careless wave of his hand. 'Oh, and the way out is through that door, just in case you're wondering. You probably missed it last time, seeing as you were in such a rush to leave.'

Spinning on his heel, he turned and walked back into the bedroom, resisting the temptation to slam the door behind him. If he hadn't been so knackered, he would have kept on walking—out of his suite and all the way to the heliport at Davos.

Frankly, it would be the only way he could guarantee that he wouldn't pull Santa into his arms and carry on from where they had left off.

Instead, he crossed the room to the decanter of whisky and poured himself a generous measure. Swearing softly, he picked up the glass, downed it in two mouthfuls and poured another.

He was quite tempted to drink the entire decanter.

A muscle ticked in his jaw. The last few hours had been some of the most baffling and frustrating of his life. If it wasn't enough that Herr Widner had interrupted them, by the time he'd finally shaken off the assistant manager and his tablet Santa had bolted.

His mouth thinned, a beat of anger pulsing over his skin. Even now he couldn't quite believe it.

Women didn't usually flee from his kisses, but Santa had done just that. One minute she was there in his arms, her body melting into him, her soft mouth fused with his, and the next—

Gone. Disappeared. Almost as if he'd imagined her.

His mouth twisted. Oh, he'd imagined her, all right— before and since. Only in his head she had mostly been naked, and always eager and frantic for his touch, not running from it.

He had been too stunned and proud to ask anyone if they had seen her, and he was only too aware of how it must look to the other guests. Louis Albemarle being stood up by a woman...

It was untenable that anyone should think he cared, or that Santa was in any way special, and so he'd forced himself to act as if she was just an *amuse-bouche* before the evening ahead.

His jaw clenched. By rights that was what she should have been.

Truthfully, he had—in part, at least—kissed her out of curiosity, out of a desire to taste her. But only to prove to himself, and her, that she wasn't special. In the main, though, he had been driven by a devilish impulse to get under her skin, to have the satisfaction of wiping that haughty, condescending look off her beautiful face.

Basically, he'd failed on both counts. And now, as if he needed any reminder of that, she was here in his suite.

Make that in his bedroom, he thought sourly, turning as Santa stalked towards him, her blue eyes narrowing accusingly.

'Where have you been? I couldn't get the door to open. There's something wrong with the lock.'

Draining his glass, he shrugged. 'Why didn't you just call Reception? They would have come and let you out.'

He watched two flags of colour rise along her cheekbones. 'I don't know. I suppose I wasn't thinking straight.'

The words came out in a rush, the colour in her cheeks deepening as she glanced at the bed, and he knew that, like him, she was remembering those mind-blowing minutes when their bodies had gone into meltdown.

Putting his empty glass down beside the decanter, he rested his eyes on her face, his muscles tensing, his body aching with an excruciating burn of frustration. A frustration that was unlikely to be eased any time soon, judging by the outrage shining in Santa's eyes.

Although, frankly, what did she have to be outraged about? She hadn't been left at a party with a head full of questions and a hard-on.

He gritted his teeth.

'Not thinking straight?' He glanced at his watch. 'Surely it didn't take you five hours to unravel your thoughts?'

That had her lifting her chin, bringing her blue eyes up to his. 'I must have fallen asleep. But I wouldn't have needed to *unravel my thoughts* anyway if you hadn't kissed me. In fact, I wouldn't even have been in your bathroom.'

Shaking his head, he held her gaze, a pulse of irritation and disbelief beating through his body. 'I might have known you'd make this my fault. Go on, then. Tell me,' he ordered, taking a step towards her. 'How am I responsible for any of this?'

She raised her chin, blue eyes flashing like a police car at the scene of a crime. 'Don't be more of a jerk than you are already. You know how… What are you doing?'

Her voice rose to an indignant squeak at the end of the sentence as he sat down heavily on the bed and began toeing off his shoe.

'Are you getting undressed?'

'Why?' He stopped what he was doing and let his gaze fix on her mouth. 'Do you want to pick up from where we left off?'

She drew in a sharp little breath, her blue eyes locking with his as she shook her head violently. 'No, I do not,' she snapped.

His shoulders tensed at the fierce conviction in her voice. *Not that he cared,* he thought savagely. Wrapped up in that gleaming satin, she might look, and taste, like the most tempting piece of candy, but there were plenty of other less aggravating ways to get a sugar rush.

'Then that makes two of us.' He forced himself to hold her gaze, as if he weren't the least bit affected by the memory of those few heated moments in the room next door. 'I think we're done here, don't you?'

Raging inside, feeling thwarted on so many levels, he began to pull his bow tie loose. He felt wrecked, and not only with alcohol. He was tired—the kind of tired that had as much to do with mood as physical fatigue—and drinking had only worsened that mood. Right now he just wanted this night—day—whatever it was—to end.

She gave him one of those delicate, needle-sharp smiles that cut to the bone. 'There is no "we", Your Grace.'

'Keep telling yourself that if you want, but it won't make it any truer.' Meeting her icy stare, he let a mocking smile pull at the corners of his mouth. 'I might have kissed you first, but as I remember it you were a fully active participant when *we* were kissing.'

And he could certainly remember it, he thought, his body stirring at the memory of how his senses had screamed to have her. Watching her chin jerk up swiftly, he knew she did too, and he let his smile grow.

'In fact, I'd go as far to say that *you* were champing at the bit.'

Two spots of colour spread across her cheeks as she shot him an icy stare. 'You can't help yourself, can you? A decent man would never be so crude, but I suppose I shouldn't be surprised—'

His eyes narrowed on her face. 'You want to talk about decency? How about we talk about you just up and vanishing without so much as a word?'

'There was nothing to say,' she protested. 'It shouldn't have happened. It was a mistake.'

'You're damned right it was. One I'm planning on forgetting asap.'

Her sharp intake of breath wrenched at something inside him, but he told himself he didn't care. She had hardly minced her words, had she?

'Now, if you don't mind, I think I'm going to quit while I'm behind and get some sleep.'

'*Sleep?*'

Now what? She was staring at him as if he'd suddenly sprouted antlers.

'No, you are *not* going to sleep, Louis.' Her voice was cold and crisp, like new fallen snow, but there was an edge to it too, almost like panic. 'I need to get out of here.'

Santa felt her heartbeat accelerate as Louis looked up at her irritably. 'So go. I'm not stopping you, am I? In fact, let me help you leave.'

Before she could react, he stood up and reached for her arm, and began frog-marching her across the bedroom.

'Let me go.' She shook him off, her anger swept aside by a rush of panic at his touch and her body's instant, indisputable response to it.

Her heart bumped against her ribs. At first when the door had opened she'd simply felt relief at being freed. Now, though, that relief had faded, and there was nothing to filter the impact of his devastating dark looks or the lean, hard lines of his body in that impeccably tailored tuxedo.

Her pulse twitched and she felt her face grow hot as she remembered the urgent press of his mouth and the heat of his hands burning through the fabric of her dress. Remembered, too, her own feverish, uninhibited reaction.

She hadn't instigated what had happened, but she'd come damn close. Another second and she would have reached up and clasped his face, pressed a desperate kiss to his mouth.

Louis was right. She might not like him, but she wanted him.

But even if that was true, what difference did it make?

Nothing had changed. She was still the same woman she had been with Nathan, and the idea of revealing her 'real' self to Louis made her stomach twist painfully.

And yet she wasn't sure she was strong enough to resist this attraction she felt for him.

Taking a step back, she folded her arms in front of her stomach defensively. 'I'm not going anywhere.'

'What are you talking about now?' His eyebrows snapped together and, shaking his dark head, he held up his hands in mock surrender. 'Okay, I'm done with this. Just go back to your room, Santa.' He stepped backwards, his blue eyes narrowed again, his fine-boned features cold and set. 'No need to say goodbye. You can just sneak off when my back's turned. You're good at that, aren't you?'

She hadn't sneaked off. She had run—run from the wild and uncontrollable passion that had flared between them. Or, more specifically, from the humiliating knowledge that she could not sustain or arouse that passion in private.

But she certainly wasn't about to share that with Louis, a man whose sexual prowess was the subject of very public record.

'I can't go to my room.' Santa stared at him, hesitating, her heart thudding. 'I don't have one.' She spoke quickly, trying to outrun the sudden nervousness zig-zagging down her spine as his eyes locked with hers. 'I'm not a guest here. I'm staying with a friend. In town.'

There was a long, pulsing silence. 'You have to be kidding me?' he said softly. He covered the space between them in three swift strides, stopping in front of her, his mouth a perfectly executed curl of contempt. A muscle ticked in his jaw. 'No wonder you didn't want to call Reception.'

'I had an invitation to the party,' she said icily.

'Just not a room at the hotel.'

Forcing herself to meet his taunting smile, she straightened her shoulders. 'No, I don't have a room. Which is why I need help to get back to the chalet.'

'So call your friend…?' He let a silence fall between them as he waited for her to provide a name.

'Merry,' she said finally, reluctantly.

'Really?' He raised one dark eyebrow. 'Okay… So call Merry, or one of Santa's other little helpers, and she can come and help you.'

Her stomach clenched. There was no way she was going to call Merry. It wasn't fair to get her friend involved in what was essentially a spectacular mess of her own making. Particularly not when that mess was happening here in the Haensli, where Merry worked.

She scowled at him. 'I can't. That's why I need your help.'

He stared at her for a beat, his blue eyes widening with incredulity, and then he must have realised she was being serious because he started laughing.

'What's so funny?' she snapped.

'You're joking, right?' His smile had transformed into something closer to a sneer. 'Why the hell should I help you?'

The panic and confusion of the last few hours

morphed into a flare of anger. Stepping towards him, she stabbed a finger against the wall of his chest. 'Because it's your fault I'm here. And because if someone sees me dressed like this, coming out of your suite, it'll look like I spent the night—' She broke off.

'*With me.*' He finished her sentence.

'Yes, with you,' she returned icily. 'And you might not care about your reputation, but I do care about mine.'

Louis didn't reply. He just stared at her in silence. And the look of contempt and disgust on his face tugged at a memory she had tried her hardest to erase—a memory that still had the power to make her feel small and stupid and tawdry.

Only why was this *her* fault? Louis was the one who had pressed the play button.

Ignoring the jittery feeling in her legs, she lifted her chin. 'As I remember it, you kissed me in front of a room full of people, so you can damn well help me now.'

His lip curled. 'And what exactly would you have me do?'

'I just need to borrow some clothes. Maybe some shoes.'

He was staring at her now as if she had suggested dressing up as a pantomime horse. 'Great idea. Yeah, I can see *that* not drawing any attention to you.'

Now that she'd said it out loud, it did sound ridiculous. Only she didn't have a Plan B.

'Is that your idea of help? Because—' she began, but he cut her off with a withering look.

'Enough, okay? There's only one possible way you're going to get downstairs without anyone seeing you. You're going to have to use the fire escape. It comes out at the side of the hotel, so you won't have to go through Reception.'

Turning, he began to walk towards the door and she stared after him, stunned by this sudden and apparently flawless solution, and by the realisation that she was finally coming to it. The moment she'd been so sure she wanted to happen.

Only now it was here, the thought that she would never see Louis again was not as comforting as she'd imagined it would be.

'I thought you were in a hurry?'

Louis's voice brought her head up with a snap. He was standing by the door, scowling, and gratefully she felt a clarifying flare of anger.

'I am,' she said.

'Then let's go,' he said irritably as she stopped in front of him.

Her heart-rate picked up as he yanked open the door, and some of her nervousness must have shown on her face because he frowned.

'Look, Santa, it's crazy to worry about your reputation.'

'Is it?' she said stiffly.

'Absolutely.' He nodded, his eyes dropping down to her shoes. 'You're probably going to break your neck in those lethal little red numbers anyway, so it won't matter.'

Louis had been right—*again*, she thought ten minutes later, as she finally reached the bottom of the fire escape. She might find skating as easy as walking, but four-inch heels and ice were not a good combination.

'I can take it from here,' she said, rubbing a hand over her arm.

After the warmth of the hotel the air felt incredibly cold, and she wasn't exactly dressed for snow. But, snow or no snow, she had to get back to the chalet. Straightening her shivering shoulders, she took a teetering step forward.

Louis held her gaze. 'That's good. Carry on like that and you should be there by lunchtime.'

Ignoring his snide tone, she took another step—and gasped as the smooth sole slipped from under her.

Louis's hand pulled her upright. Her heart beat in double-quick time and she jerked out of his grip, almost losing her footing again.

He swore softly. 'You are the most stubborn woman I've ever met. Just take my arm. In fact, take this too.'

Muttering something under his breath, he shrugged out of his jacket and draped it over her shoulders. It was heavy, and knowing that the heat of his skin was now warming her body felt oddly intimate. As she slipped her arms into the silk-lined sleeves she felt suddenly light-headed, imagining how it would feel to have Louis's warm body on hers. Beside her. Inside her.

That thought effectively silenced her for the next ten minutes as they slipped and slid over the snow-covered pavements.

'This is it,' Santa said, glancing up at Merry's small chalet. She could see there were no lights on inside and she felt a flutter of relief. She had done it, and without having to bother Merry.

She shrugged out of his jacket and handed it back to him. The sudden chill made her skin tighten and she felt suddenly ridiculously bereft, as if she had lost something personal and important.

'Thank you,' she said quickly. 'For walking me back.''

His eyes locked with hers and for a second they both stared at each other, their warm breath curling through the cool air. Then he reached out and gently touched her earlobe.

She saw it in his eyes at the same time as she felt it low in her belly. A flicker of heat—needle-sharp and impossible to ignore. And suddenly what had happened last night didn't feel like a mistake any more.

'You missed out on your goodie bag. Have it as an early Christmas present on me,' he said softly. 'Just don't tell anyone. I don't want my bad boy reputation ruined.'

Heart pounding, she watched as he turned and walked slowly back down the street.

Inside the chalet it was blissfully warm. Slipping off her shoes, she crept into her room and closed the door. She was incredibly tired and, undressing quickly, she slid under the covers.

But as soon as she lay down she felt suddenly and unaccountably wide awake.

She breathed in deeply. Usually if she couldn't sleep she worked through her routines in her head, tracing out the patterns on the ice. Only today her head wouldn't cooperate. She exhaled shakily. Instead, and for no good or logical reason, all she could see was Louis's glittering blue eyes, watching her intently as his hands traced patterns on her naked body.

* * *

What the—?

Rolling over, Louis grabbed a pillow and pressed it over his head. Who the hell was ringing his room?

Head pounding, he gritted his teeth, waiting for it to stop.

Thank goodness.

As the room fell silent he reached over and irritably pulled the phone jack out of the wall, falling back against the pillow with a grunt.

Only now he was awake.

He kept his eyes closed. He was not ready to wake up and face the world. A world that suddenly seemed very dull.

But why? Nothing had changed.

He was still the Duke of Astbury. He was still the CEO of a global jewellery brand with an A-list clientele. And after the success of last night's goodie bag rollout he was almost certainly one step closer to reaching his goal of being able to buy out the shareholders.

Only for some reason that didn't seem to matter quite as much this morning as it had every other morning for the last six months.

He frowned up at the ceiling. It made no sense for him to feel like that. He'd pretty much curtailed his entire life to make that goal. So why suddenly had his priorities been shifted?

Not shifted, he thought irritably. *Diverted.*

Derailed. By Santa.

Grimacing, he sat up and swung his legs out of bed. Normally if he wanted a woman it was just a question of when and where and how often. But with Santa the answers to those questions were, frustratingly, *never*, *nowhere* and *zero*—in that order.

And that was why he was feeling like this. Especially after what had happened last night. Or rather what hadn't happened.

His heart began to pound against his ribs as he remembered how panicky Santa had been about being seen with him.

Could she really be that bothered about her reputation? He felt his shoulders tense sharply. Or was there another reason for her not wanting even a whisper of scandal? Did she have some man at home? A faithful lover waiting in the wings for his skater girl?

The thought of some anonymous man holding Santa in his arms, of her hands splayed over his back, guiding his movements, cut like the flick of a knife.

Not that he cared *per se* about her sex life, he told himself quickly. Santa wasn't special. No woman would ever be that again—he'd learned his lesson with Marina.

Nor was she even his type. She was snippy and stubborn and far too judgemental for him. He knew he could have any woman he wanted. The only reason he wanted her—the only logical reason—was because he couldn't have her.

His mouth twisted. Sexual frustration—that was what this feeling was. And once he'd left Klosters he'd forget all about Santa Somerville and her endless legs, lustrous dark hair and lush mouth—

Scowling as his groin hardened, he stood up and began tugging his shirt free. He'd been too tired this morning to undress before he fell into bed, so was it surprising that he couldn't shake off this mood? He was still in yesterday's clothes—therefore he was still in yesterday's headspace.

But that was nothing a shower and breakfast in bed followed by an hour or two on the slopes couldn't fix.

Wandering back into the bedroom ten minutes later, he felt one hundred percent better. Now all he needed was a plate of Eggs Benedict and some black coffee and he would be ready to take on the windy black run down to the village of Wolfgang.

He was about to pick up the phone and call Room Service when he remembered he had switched off his own phone last night. Nick would probably be climbing the walls.

Should he call him?

He didn't want to ruin his breakfast.

But why should it be ruined? He'd drunk a lot last night, mainly to blot out the pulse of hunger still beating a path around his body. But other than that he'd been a model guest, no housekeeping required. Better still, practically every woman at the party had been wearing Callière diamond earrings—including two princesses and several members of rock royalty.

No, for once, Nick would be singing his praises. And to his surprise he found that he was actually looking forward to speaking to his CMO.

When he switched on his phone, twenty messages pinged into his inbox. Nineteen were from Nick. One was from Donald Muir, the most exacting of his shareholders. Clearly news of his success had travelled fast.

Just as he was congratulating himself the phone rang, and probably for the first time in his life he answered it right away.

'Nick—how are you this fine morning?' Sprawling back on the bed, he switched his phone to speaker. He wanted to hear this loud and clear.

'How do you *think* I am?'

As Nick's voice boomed into the bedroom Louis felt his whole body tense. He'd been expecting his CMO to sound jubilant—euphoric, even. Instead he sounded furious.

'I thought you'd be happy...' he said slowly. Was this some kind of elaborate joke?

There was a stunned silence at the other end of the phone. Then, 'Happy? Why on earth would I be happy, Louis?'

He heard Nick swear, and immediately he sobered up. No matter how annoyed or exasperated he'd been over the years, he'd never heard his CMO swear.

'You know, I have been your biggest, your only cheerleader. I've made excuses. I've covered your arse. And this is how you repay me—' Losing control of his voice, Nick broke off.

Louis frowned. A flicker of unease slid down his spine. 'What are you talking about?'

'I'm talking about your one-night stand with the ice cream girl.'

'Santa?' He sat up slowly, his heart beating out of time.

'Yes, Santa. The skater. Bryson's Ices. Little Miss Squeaky Clean.'

'I know who she is, Nick,' Louis said coolly.

'I should hope so, given that you spent the night with her.'

'No, that's not—' he began.

But Nick cut him off. 'Save it for someone who doesn't know you, Louis.'

He heard his CMO groan.

'I can't believe you could be so stupid. What on earth possessed you to hook up with that particular woman? And at the Haensli party, of all places.'

'I didn't hook up with her,' he said hotly. 'That's not what happened.'

'So you *didn't* kiss her in front of a whole bunch of people at a party in your room?'

Louis felt his chest tighten. To say that this conversation was not going as he'd planned would be the mother of all understatements. In fact, it had gone completely off-piste.

'It was just a kiss, Nick.'

'So you didn't see her after that?' his CMO persisted.

'No… Well, yes… But it's not what you think—'

'You don't get it, do you?' Nick interrupted him again. 'It's not what I think that matters here. It's what the shareholders think. It's what the public thinks. Look at the photos, Louis. Oh, and while you're at it you might want to watch the video too.'

Video! His shoulders stiffened with shock. *What video?*

Standing up, he walked across the room and flipped open his laptop. He hesitated, then typed in his own name.

His breathing stalled as he stared down at the screen. *The Duke of Hazard!*

That was the caption above a picture of Santa clutching his arm at the top of the fire escape.

No, this couldn't be happening.

What was more, it hadn't actually happened.

Only nobody was going to believe that, looking at these photos.

Somebody must have snapped them with a phone. They were not paparazzi standard, but they were still clear enough to see his face, and Santa's.

He scrolled down the page, his heartbeat accelerating.

Quite a few of them had been taken when they were on the fire escape, with Santa wearing his jacket and the two of them clutching one another conspiratorially. Then there were a few more of them in the street, with her arm tucked under his, and even one just after she'd slipped again, and he had ended up anchoring her against his body.

Most incriminating of all were the pictures of him and Santa outside her friend's chalet. They were standing staring at one another and there was something oddly intimate about their posture, even though in reality the photo must have been taken just moments before she gave him back his jacket.

All of it could be explained away.

But who would believe his explanations?

He found the video easily enough. It had been taken at that party in Cannes—he recognised what he was wearing. But what he was wearing wasn't the problem. It was what he was saying.

'I'm always in love. That's why I'm not married.'

It was his take on the Oscar Wilde quote. He'd been playing to the crowd. But now, playing back the audio, he felt his mouth thin as he listened to the conceit his voice and the hoots of appreciative laughter in the background.

Even to his ears it sounded bad.

He felt a sharp, unfamiliar stab of panic. 'Have the shareholders seen this?'

But even before Nick's terse affirmation he knew that they had. That was why Donald Muir had called him.

He swore silently.

'What are they thinking?' he asked quietly.

'They can't understand why a man who runs a business that's so inextricably tied to love and romance and marriage would make that kind of remark in public.'

Louis breathed out unsteadily. His heart was beating too fast. 'It was a private party, Nick, and it was months ago.'

There was another silence, this time longer. Then, 'They want you to step down as CEO.'

'No!' The word burst from his mouth. 'No, they can't ask me to do that. They can't make me do that.'

'They can and they will.' Nick hesitated, his voice softening. 'Look, I know how much you care about Callière, but these last few months you've been out of control. They think you're a loose cannon.'

Louis felt his chest tighten. He wanted to explain— to tell Nick why it wasn't his fault. Tell him that his father's death had unleashed something in him…an anger and a pain that was beyond his control.

But he couldn't admit that to anyone.

He couldn't admit the depth of his hurt or his regret at not confronting his father. Or that he needed Nick's help. He could never admit to that.

'There's got to be something I can do or say.'

His CMO sighed. 'You know what, Louis? I think you've said and done enough, don't you? Look, don't answer your phone unless it's me. Don't leave your room. And don't, under any circumstances whatsoever, talk to Santa Somerville.'

As Nick hung up, Louis slammed his laptop shut.

Santa Somerville. This was her fault. None of this would have happened if she hadn't run off and got herself stuck in his bathroom, and then badgered him into walking her home.

For the last ten years his business—the business he had built from scratch, the business that bore his beloved grandmother's name—had been the one constant in his life. After Glamma's death, his need to own it outright had become almost an obsession, and he'd been so close.

Only now it was hanging in the balance.

All those months of being on his best behaviour had been for nothing. Thanks to Santa. And now he had been told to stay in his room like some disobedient child.

A sick feeling balled in his stomach. He'd been here before. And back then he hadn't been able to do it... play the game. He couldn't believe that he was expected to do so again.

His muscles tensed. The memory of that conversation was still raw. How could it not be? It had defined his life. He was still living with the consequences of it now.

But now, as then, he couldn't just sit here and wait for his life to be decided for him.

As for not talking to Santa?

Not going to happen.
He was going to find her and talk to her.
And, whatever it took, she was going to put this right.

CHAPTER FIVE

GAZING UP AT the cloudless forget-me-not-blue sky, Santa breathed in deeply.

She had woken just over half an hour ago, disorientated to discover that it was past lunchtime.

It was the longest lie-in of her entire life, and she had been expecting Merry to already be up, but there was no sign of her friend, nor was there a note, so she must still be sleeping.

A prickle of guilt jabbed beneath her ribs. She had chosen not to knock on Merry's door, telling herself that her friend needed her rest, but that wasn't the reason she hadn't woken her.

The truth was Merry would know in a heartbeat that something had happened last night, and right now Santa wasn't sure she could even explain it to herself, much less anyone else, and particularly not to her best friend.

At the very least she needed a chance to process everything…a few moments alone to decide which parts of last night and this morning she would share with her. So she got dressed, left a note on the kitchen counter saying that she was going for a walk, and then quietly sneaked out of the chalet.

She was glad that she had; it was a beautiful day. The air was cold—refreshingly so—and the sun looked like a giant white snowball, just hovering over the town.

Having forgotten to draw the curtains, she had woken to that same sun, its pure white light pressing against her eyelids and pulling her from sleep.

Not that she had minded. In fact, she had been happy to wake.

A dull heat rose over her face.

Louis might have walked away from the chalet early this morning, but if her dreams were anything to go by he hadn't really left her.

On the contrary, he had been right there beside her, his hard, muscular body pressed close to hers in Merry's small fold-out bed, his mouth on her mouth, his skin on her skin, his hands touching, exploring, teasing her, making her shift restlessly against the weight of the duvet.

The jingling of bells from a horse-drawn sleigh dragged her back into real time and, cheeks still warm, she watched the two grey horses jog rather than dash through the snow, their heads held high.

It was unsettling as well as embarrassing to know that whatever she might have said to Louis's face, her subconscious had been busily undermining her, treacherously unleashing her unfiltered, inhibited desires and wishes during sleep.

But surely that was the point of dreams? They weren't real. And the Louis in her dreams wasn't real either. She had made him up. He was a fantasy.

Her mouth thinned. The real Louis might look like every woman's dream lover, with his floppy brown hair, perfect bone structure and teasing blue eyes, but looks weren't everything, and no woman, no matter how smitten, wanted a sulky, spoiled, self-indulgent boy for a lover.

There was a soft thump as a slab of snow slid from the roof of one of the chalets onto the ground.

She frowned. It must have snowed while she was sleeping, but it was still easier to walk along the pavements now than earlier, when she'd been clinging to Louis's arm to stop herself from falling flat on her face.

Her pulse skipped several beats.

She couldn't believe that she'd had the nerve to do it—that she'd actually come out and asked…no, *demanded* his help. But, with hindsight, what was more surprising was that Louis had helped her above and beyond what she'd expected him to.

Truthfully, as soon as she'd reached the bottom of the fire escape he could simply have left her and let her slip and slide her way home. He hadn't needed to lend her his jacket, or walk her back to Merry's, and yet he had done both of those things—begrudgingly at first, but by the time they'd reached the chalet his mood had shifted. The sulky boy had vanished and his arm around her waist had felt completely normal.

Right.

Perfect.

Her heart clenched.

Just like the kiss they'd shared.

She breathed in sharply, remembering the heat of his mouth and the urgent press of his body. Remembering, too, her own feverish response.

That had been real—

Her throat tightened. Except it hadn't been.

Obviously it had been real in the sense that it had happened, but no matter how mind-blowingly passionate it had been that kiss wasn't who she was. Whoever she had been in those few heated moments…it wasn't her.

The real Santa Somerville was disappointingly clumsy and tame. In other words, a real let-down.

She swallowed, her heart pounding, a shiver of misery snaking down her spine. She even had the photo to prove it, so there was no point in pretending otherwise.

It had been just a kiss, nothing to make a fuss about, and the right and the only thing to do was to put it behind her. Act as if it had never happened. The whole episode, including her shockingly intense reaction, was best forgotten.

Louis was best forgotten too.

And that shouldn't be too difficult, she told herself quickly. There was no reason why she should see him again. They were from different worlds; it was a miracle that they had even met in the first place.

She was lucky they had kissed in his suite. Only a few of his guests had seen them, and they weren't the kind of people who would care, or tell, and nobody knew that she'd spent the night in his bathroom. It was just between the two of them.

Looking up, she frowned. She wasn't sure why, but she had unthinkingly made her way to the hotel. And it looked as if something was happening.

There was a whole bunch of paparazzi hanging around outside the entrance, all blowing on their hands and chattering excitedly. A celebrity worth snapping must be arriving or leaving.

But she'd had enough of the rich and the famous to last her, if not a lifetime, at least until she left Klosters.

And now that she had got her head straight, she was going to get some pastries from one of the little bakeries in town and treat Merry to breakfast in bed.

'There she is... *Santa!*'

She didn't recognise the voice, but jerked her head upwards automatically at the sound of her name. And before she had time to blink the paparazzi turned as one. For a few dazed half-seconds her brain kept telling her eyes that they were looking at someone else, but then they surged towards her, and suddenly everyone was calling her name.

Blinded by camera flashes, she felt as if she had stepped into a film—a terrifying film where nothing made sense.

Everyone was shouting at her, their questions overlapping, jumbling inside her head, so that it was impossible to understand what they were saying, and she was having to concentrate even more than she had earlier that morning to keep upright as they jostled one another to get closer.

She had to get out of there.

It was her last conscious thought before the clamouring pack of reporters and photographers swarmed forward and surrounded her and she acted on it, trying to push her way through to freedom. But there were too many of them.

And then, just as her shock began crumbling into panic, Louis was there, shoving his way through the mob, his broad shoulders making easy work of their cameras and microphones, and even the pushiest photographer falling away from his fulminating expression. He grabbed her hand, shielding her with his body as the hotel's security team swept past them, and then they were inside the Haensli.

'Louis, what is—?'

'Not here,' he snapped, his scowl scattering staff and guests alike as he hauled her through the lobby into the lift.

'Yes, here,' she said, yanking her hand out of his, her panic forgotten, anger sluicing through her veins as the doors closed. 'What the hell is going on?'

'What's going on?' he repeated, staring at her in disbelief. 'How can you not know? Haven't you looked at your phone this morning?'

Her heart was beating heavily in her chest. Outside, she had thought he was furious with the press. In fact, just for a moment, she had actually toyed with the idea that he was rescuing her.

Now, though, staring at his curled lip and taut, stubble-covered jaw, she realised that he was furious with her.

But why? And what did he mean about looking at her phone?

She felt a shiver of foreboding scuttle down her backbone as the lift doors opened and he strode through them into the hallway.

Heart thumping against her ribs, she followed him into his suite. 'No, I haven't,' she said. She had put it in her jacket pocket, but been too busy unpicking the events of the last twenty-four hours to even check for messages. 'Why, has something happened?

'A lot.' He spun round, his blue eyes glittering like polished gemstones. 'While you've been sleeping, my beauty, you and I have become an item.'

What? Santa blinked. She and Louis barely knew one another. They certainly weren't an item.

'I—I don't understand,' she stammered, her voice higher than usual.

His face hardened. 'You will,' he said curtly, picking up a laptop and flipping it open.

She grabbed the back of a chair to steady herself, a slithering panic crawling over her skin. 'Do you think I told someone that you kissed me? Because I didn't. I haven't told anyone—'

He gazed down at her incredulously.

'You think that's why the paparazzi are camped out on the doorstep of the Haensli? Because of one stupid, meaningless little kiss?'

Her fingers bit into the leather edge of the chair and she stared at him, wounded not just by his careless dismissal of what had felt so astonishing and intoxicating to her, but by her own outsized sense of misery that he felt that way.

She let the air out of her lungs carefully, then took another breath. 'But that's all that happened.'

Now he was staring at her as if she had told him she believed in the Abominable Snowman.

'Believe it or not, they don't know about the kiss. But they don't need to know.' He was biting the words off and spitting them out. 'Because—idiot that I am—I agreed to walk you home this morning and now they have something much, much better than a kiss. But if you don't believe me, take a look.'

Louis held up the laptop and, glancing down, everything she was thinking and feeling was swept away.

She felt the room grow hazy around her as she scrolled down the screen.

Snow Queen melts for Duke of Diamonds!

Santa, baby...hurry down my fire escape tonight!

Her head was spinning, a wordless protest building in her throat, and then her phone buzzed, and she clicked on the message, and what she saw made a chasm open up beneath her feet.

She was falling down into darkness...

Watching the colour drain away from her face, Louis swore silently.

In the time it had taken for him to yank on his clothes and slam his hand against the lift button he'd cooled down sufficiently to know that he was acting like a jerk, blaming Santa for the mess he was in.

He'd also begun thinking that, despite what Nick had said, there might be a chance he could swing this just by lying low. Stories like this were tomorrow's chip wrappers. With no new oxygen to feed them, they would quickly die.

His breathing knotted.

Only then he'd seen the paps outside, and everything had suddenly got real, and he'd known that this story was alive and kicking and that once again he was going to be blamed for something he hadn't done.

It was all so horribly familiar, and he had felt the same sickening sense of disbelief and helplessness. His rage and frustration that it was happening all over again, just like it had with Marina, had risen up like a wave, swamping everything.

And now, glancing over at the photos on his laptop screen, he felt an outlet for his anger as his eyes locked on to that expression on her face as if she only had eyes for him.

He was suddenly conscious of the hammering of his heart. How could she do that? How could she look at a man like that and not mean it? He'd thought she was different. She had seemed so different when he'd kissed her…so eager and lacking in artifice.

But she was just like every other woman, and for some reason that hurt a ridiculous amount, so that he couldn't keep the bitterness out of his voice as he met her gaze.

'Do you have any idea what you've done?' he said coldly. 'It's taken ten years, but finally everything was falling into place. I was this close…' He held up his hand, his thumb and forefinger spaced an inch apart. 'This close to being able to buy out my shareholders. And then you came along, with your swishy hair and your ice skates, and messed it all up. And now they want me to take a step back.'

There was a long, taut silence and then Santa gazed up at him. 'I came along and *messed it all up*?' she repeated, the blazing fury in her voice more than matching his. 'You did this. All of this is your fault.' She held up her phone with a shaking hand. 'Bryson's are furious. They're threatening to pull my sponsorship.'

Louis stared at her in silence, his pulse filling his head. He was being pushed out of his own company, the company he had built out of the hard Canadian ground, and she was worrying about her sponsorship?

But there was something in her voice…something in the way she was holding herself—almost as if she had been waiting for the sky to fall on her head—and he didn't like the way that made him feel.

'That's not going to happen.'

Why would it? Unlike him, Santa had never put a foot wrong, on or off the ice, but he felt obliged to say it…to say something to make her relax.

'It'll be okay,' he said briskly.

Her chin jerked up and she glared at him. 'How? Bryson's made it clear when I signed the contract that my behaviour had to be consistent with their brand image, and your reputation isn't exactly family-friendly.'

Eyes narrowing, Louis stared at her in exasperation. Really? Was this the thanks he got for trying to be nice?

'Well, maybe you should have thought of that when you decided to drag me into your walk of shame.'

Her hands clenched by her sides. 'That's not what it was, and you know it.'

They were inches apart, both of them breathing jerkily. The air around them swirled and swelled with anger and resentment, and something else that seemed to push them closer, so that he could smell the faint trace of her perfume, see the pulse chasing down her throat—

A shrill ringtone broke into the silence filling the

room and they both jerked backwards. As Santa stared down at her phone, he watched her face still.

He frowned. 'Who is it?'

She was staring at the phone, stiffly frozen, appalled, as if she was holding a live rattlesnake. 'It's Diana. My agent.'

Before his brain had a chance to catch up with his body, Louis stretched out a hand and grabbed the phone from her. He switched it off.

'What are you doing?' Her eyes flew to his face. 'I need to call her back.'

'And say what?' His frown turned into a scowl. 'That nothing happened?' He gestured towards the open laptop and the picture of Santa wearing his tuxedo jacket, her body leaning familiarly into his in the empty snow-covered street. 'That it was all perfectly innocent?'

'It was.'

For a moment, he almost felt sorry for her. She sounded defiant, but her face was pale, the muscles taut, as if she were trying not to panic. And he knew exactly how she was feeling because he was feeling it too.

The difference was that he'd been here before, whereas this was her first time, and the first time was definitely the worst.

His stomach twisted. He could still remember now how it had been after he'd jilted Marina at the wedding of the decade. It had been like a crazy dream. For weeks, months, his name and face had been plastered over every news outlet in the world. He'd been hounded, harassed and hunted across the globe.

There was an ache in his chest like a bruise that had never healed. And the people who should have protected him, taken him in, given him sanctuary, had not just turned their backs…they had pushed him into the abyss.

He glanced over at Santa's set face.

But that wasn't going to happen this time.

'You think people care about whether you're innocent or guilty, Santa? They don't. You think they care about whether things are true or not? They don't. All they want is a juicy story.' His eyes found hers. 'And we have given them one.'

'I told you before, there is no "we".'

She met his eyes fiercely, even though he could see from the faint tremor of her body that she was fighting to stay calm.

'There is now,' he said grimly.

'No!'

The word burst from her mouth just as it had done from his earlier, when Nick had told him that the shareholders wanted him to take a step back from the business.

'We just need to tell them to take these pictures down and print a retraction—'

'Who?' His eyes narrowed on her flushed, angry face. 'Who are we going to tell? That's not how the internet works. These pictures have been shared hundreds of thousands of times already.'

Even if they could be taken down—which he doubted—the damage had already been done. Any explanation they offered now was already too little, too late. It might even make them look more guilty.

Not that Santa would accept that.

He could almost see her picking through his words, turning them over and upside down, looking for some kind of loophole that would make all this go away. He felt something pinch inside him as she twisted abruptly away from him.

He swore under his breath. 'Santa—'

She didn't reply, and her silence went on so long that he began to think she had nothing more to say. But then she turned to face him.

'I need this sponsorship, Louis.' Her eyes were very blue. 'I'm not like you. I didn't get handed piles of money just because of who I am. And skating at my level costs a lot of money.'

'Now, you listen to me—' he began. But before he could tell her that, sadly, he hadn't been handed any piles of money in a long time, she cut him off.

'No, you listen to *me*,' she snapped. 'You started this and you're going to finish it. I don't care what you have to do or say to make those headlines go away, but that's what needs to happen.'

'Oh, why didn't you say?' He patted his jacket, as if searching for something. 'If that's all that needs to happen, I'll just find my magic wand and use my special headline-shrinking spell. While I'm at it, I could give the entire world amnesia too.'

Rubbing his forehead, where an ache was starting to build, he watched fury flicker across Santa's face.

'I wish I'd never met you.'

'Likewise!' he flung back at her.

His heart began to thud rhythmically in his chest. What the hell was she expecting him to do? Without access to a time machine, the only way he could make those headlines disappear would be if and Santa were a real couple—

He tensed, a fragment of a sentence echoing inside his head.

'I'm getting tired of trying to convince the world that your behaviour is the sign of a desperately romantic man searching for the right woman.'

They were Nick's words, spoken sarcastically on the day he'd arrived in Klosters.

But, then again, those words might offer a lifeline…

He was suddenly aware of the woman standing in front of him, and of what he was contemplating with her.

Ten years ago he had jilted the woman he was supposed to marry, leaving her standing at the altar in front of nine hundred carefully selected guests. And he had never regretted it—never once considered offering his name to any other woman.

Until now.

His gaze took in her shiny dark ponytail, trembling mouth and furious blue eyes. It was a crazy idea. It would never work. She would never agree to it. He didn't even want to suggest it. But, despite all the objections ringing in his ears, he knew it was the only solution to their problem.

'You said you wanted this to be over…' He paraphrased her words, watching her eyes lift warily to his face.

'I do.' Her reply was swift and clear and unequivocal.

He held her gaze, wanting to see her reaction. 'Care to say that for real?'

'What does that mean?'

He took a breath, trying to check the misgivings

clamouring inside his head. 'You want to make the headlines go away, Santa? Then marry me.'

Santa stared at him, groping for some way for his words to make sense.

Marry him!

But of course he was being stupid again—mocking her, trying to punish her for what he saw as a problem of her making.

'Good idea,' she snapped. 'Why don't we fly to Vegas? We could get married with Elvis as the celebrant and afterwards we could invite all our new paparazzi friends to the reception.'

His face hardened. 'If you like—although I thought the whole point of getting married was to get them off our backs.'

She felt her face dissolve, her mouth forming an O of shock. He was being serious. 'Are you out of your mind?'

Marry Louis? The idea was absurd, and wrong on so many levels, and yet she couldn't stop a hectic pulse from leapfrogging across her skin, or deflect a sudden vivid memory of the moment when his mouth had fused with hers.

'No!' Shaking her head to clear the image from her head, she took a step backwards. 'I wouldn't marry you if my life depended on it.'

'What about your reputation?'

His voice was cold—but, looking into his eyes, she saw the heat of wounded male pride.

Louis's pride was the last of her worries right now.

'We can't get married,' she said firmly.

'Why not?' he shot back. 'It would solve our immediate problems. Unless, of course, you're already married.'

His eyes locked with hers and she stiffened. 'I'm not married.'

'And you don't have a boyfriend right now, do you?'

Her cheeks were flaming with a shame she hated feeling. 'I would hardly have kissed you if I did.'

Something shifted in his face—something she hadn't got a name for.

'It's not always an obstacle,' he said silkily.

'Only for someone like you.'

'If you say so.'

He tilted his head back, the coldness in his eyes making her shake inside.

'Okay then, as there appears to be no legal impediment as to why I, Louis, may not be joined in matrimony to you, Santa Somerville, let's get married.'

She stared at him, trying and failing to read his expression. No legal impediment maybe, but what about a moral one?

'You can't just use marriage as some kind of sticking plaster to fix this mess.'

He shrugged. 'That's exactly what I want to use it for.'

Her head was starting to spin. *Why was he being so contrary?*

'Well, I don't. It would be dishonest, wrong—'

'It would also be expedient and mutually beneficial. And it's not as if it's going to be till-death-us-do-part. We'll be lucky if we last a month without killing each other.'

And what about kissing each other?

She felt her body still as she imagined what it would be like to share this man's bed, to have unlimited freedom to explore and savour his body—

Except that wasn't going to happen.

'People don't marry to get the paparazzi off their backs, Louis.'

'People marry for all sorts of reasons, Santa. Love…' his eyes met hers, and the blueness of his taunting gaze made her breath catch in her throat '…money, duty, convenience. And what could be more convenient than you and I getting our lives back on track?'

Her heart stopped beating. It was a crazy idea. It would never work. But what was the alternative? She could switch on her phone and call Diana and tell her the truth… Only this was one of those occasions when the truth would sound even more far-fetched than the lie.

'I don't know…'

She could hear the uncertainty in her voice, feel the lump in her throat as she swallowed.

'Do you have a better idea?'

Louis was staring down at her, his face lightly tanned from winter trips to St Barts, his aristocratic cheekbones gleaming in the afternoon sunlight.

Up close, his beauty was almost absurd—and dangerous. But not as absurd and dangerous as his proposal.

She shivered inside and then, looking into his eyes, shook her head.

CHAPTER SIX

THE HELICOPTER TILTED SHARPLY, climbing above the snow-covered Canadian landscape. Gripping her armrests, Santa shifted in her seat, a pinch of nervous tension tightening her stomach. But her nerves had nothing to do with the bumpiness of the flight.

That shake of her head had been just under forty-eight hours ago, and the reason she felt so nervous was that at some point in between then and now she had not only agreed to Louis's insane plan, she had gone ahead and married him.

And now she was no longer plain Santa Somerville, but Santa Albemarle, the Duchess of Astbury.

As she twisted the plain, gold band on her finger, her gaze flicked across the cabin of the helicopter to where her husband was slumped in his seat, apparently asleep, oblivious both to the helicopter's juddering progress and his new wife's gaze.

But she had a strong suspicion he was faking it, so that he didn't have to talk to her.

He had been like that ever since they'd left Switzerland. Not angry outwardly—he hadn't been that since they had agreed to marry—but she could sense his fury and frustration. And, even though he had sprung the trap himself, she knew he blamed her.

And she blamed him, so they were even.

Except they weren't.

Louis might be able to live with all this drama, but her head was still spinning with shock and disbelief.

Everything had happened so fast. She wondered if the details of all marriages were so quickly and easily agreed upon. Her mouth twisted. Or did that only happen when the bride and groom didn't love one another?

Somehow Louis had conjured up a private jet, and as soon as they were in the air they had each made a few phone calls. Louis had called his chief marketing officer and one of the shareholders. She had rung Diana and her family.

Diana had sounded stunned, and despite their strenuous efforts to sound thrilled she would have had to be deaf or deluded not to hear the bewilderment in her father's and stepmother's voices.

And then Mr Bryson had called her.

Her chest tightened. But of course, Mr Bryson had been truly delighted by the news that she had fallen head over heels in love.

Perhaps remembering her earlier remark, Louis had suggested they marry in Vegas. It wouldn't have been her first choice, but she had no memory of the wedding anyway, other than of how much it hurt to smile when you didn't feel like smiling.

And now they were on their way to Louis's home somewhere near Banff for their honeymoon.

Honeymoon.

Her breath caught in her throat, the word whispering

inside her. But before it had a chance to grow louder Louis's eyes snapped open, and he glanced out of the window as the helicopter started to slow.

'We're here,' he said curtly as they landed on the snow.

He soon had the door open and, barely giving her time to gaze up at the beautiful low, linear house, he hustled her across the snow. Inside, a tall, dark-haired woman with a ballerina's poise was waiting in the light-filled entrance hall beside a tall Christmas tree, decorated in minimalist style with just simple white lights and garlands of tiny pinecones.

'Welcome home, sir.' She turned to Santa and smiled. 'Welcome to Palmer's Point.'

'This is Maggie.' Louis turned to look at her, and Santa felt her stomach go into freefall. Aside from at the wedding, it was the first time he had looked at her properly in days, and she had forgotten what it felt like to be the object of that teasing blue gaze.

For a few half-seconds she pictured him stepping closer, his mouth slanting over hers, and the idea produced such a rush of longing that she missed Maggie's reply.

Her heartbeat stumbled.

How had this happened?

How had she ended up here, in this house, with this man? It might only be for a year, but right now that felt like a year too long.

'Maggie, this is my beautiful wife, Santa. Maggie runs the house for me,' Louis continued. 'You need something—anything at all—she's the person to ask. Now, I thought you might like a tour of the house...'

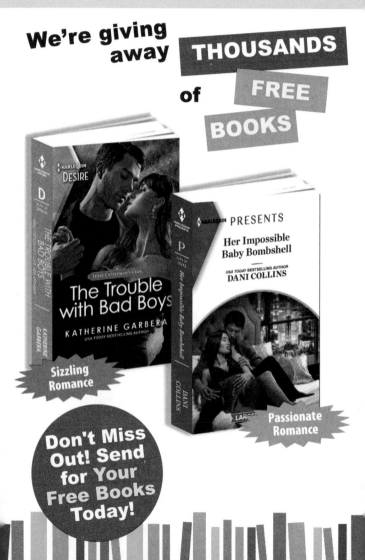

LOYAL READER
FREE BOOKS VOUCHER

YES! I Love Reading, please send me up to 4 FREE BOOKS and Free Mystery Gifts from the series I select.

Just write in "YES" on the dotted line below then return this card today and we'll send your free books & gifts asap!

➡️ YES ⬅️
- - - -

Which do you prefer?

☐ **Harlequin Desire®**
225/326 HDL GRGA

☐ **Harlequin Presents® Larger Print**
176/376 HDL GRGA

☐ **BOTH**
225/326 & 176/376 HDL GRGM

FIRST NAME

LAST NAME

ADDRESS

APT.#

CITY

STATE/PROV.

ZIP/POSTAL CODE

EMAIL ☐ Please check this box if you would like to receive newsletters and promotional emails from Harlequin Enterprises ULC and its affiliates. You can unsubscribe anytime.

HD/HP-520-LR21

No, what she would like—what she needed—was a few moments away from Louis. A few moments to come to terms with the reality of what she'd agreed to.

She cleared her throat. 'Actually, what I'd really like is to freshen up first. Perhaps you could show me to my room?'

'You mean *our* room,' he said softly.

Santa felt her heart start to beat heavily as his eyes locked with hers momentarily, before snapping back to his housekeeper's face.

'Thanks, Maggie. I think I've got this.'

Grabbing Santa by the hand, he marched her up the wide staircase, stopping as they reached the top step.

'What the hell are you playing at?' he demanded.

'I'm not playing at anything,' she snapped, pulling her hand free.

Only it didn't make any difference. Her skin felt hot where his fingers had grasped hers, as if his touch had left a permanent mark.

She felt her pulse accelerate. Without either of them saying or doing anything she could feel the mood shifting, feel herself softening towards him, the hard, cold shard of resentment and distrust starting to melt.

A rush of panic rose up inside her. She needed that splinter of ice to stay cool and distant, to keep the treacherous possibility of the two of them being transformed from enemies to lovers out of reach.

Louis stared down at her, his blue eyes narrowing. 'Really? Because you seem a little confused.'

She lifted her chin. 'I'm not confused.'

'Then what's with all the "my" room business?'

Santa looked up at him incredulously, her heart

throbbing in her throat, his question and all that it implied sending a flurry of small flames flickering across her skin.

'What did you think? That I was going to share your room?' Her voice was fraying, she was almost shouting, and she knew that she sounded a little unhinged, but she didn't care. Better that than for Louis to sense the buzz of excitement that the thought produced. 'That I was going to share your bed?'

'That is generally what husbands and wives do,' he said curtly.

'Not this husband and wife. This is a marriage of convenience, Louis.' Lifting her chin, she held his gaze. 'That means we only act like we're married when we're in public. In private, I have my own room. So either you show me where it is, or I will go and ask Maggie. Your choice, Your Grace!'

Scowling down at his laptop, Louis shifted in his top-spec ergonomic chair and then, swearing softly, leaned back and banged his head in a most unergonomic way against the headrest.

He should be feeling on top of the world.

Nick had practically wept with happiness when he'd told him he was getting married, and the shareholders had been equally delighted. Donald Muir had even sent his private jet to transport 'the happy couple' to their wedding in Vegas.

Even the media had done a complete one-eighty and, despite having portrayed him as an amoral aristocratic heartbreaker for the last ten years, were now enthusiastically recasting him as a lovesick Romeo who had just been desperately searching for his Juliet.

Catching sight of his wedding ring, he felt his scowl deepen. So pretty much across-the-board euphoria, then.

But they weren't the ones trapped in a marriage of convenience.

Nor were they spending the first day of their honeymoon wading through geological surveys.

Not that he'd done much wading, he thought, glancing down at his blank screen. He couldn't concentrate. Instead—and this was a first—his brain just kept worrying away at the thought that he had finally taken a step too far.

Maybe he should have fronted out the scandal like he had in the past. And probably he would have done if it had been just about him. But that would have meant throwing Santa under the proverbial bus...

Picturing her furious, flushed face, he lost the thread of his thoughts for a moment—and then, catching sight of the framed photograph on his desk, his own face tensed, his breathing suddenly uneven.

He wasn't doing all this for the beautiful, angry woman who now shared his name, but for another, equally beautiful woman, whose own legendary hot temper was now just a memory.

His throat tightened. He had other photos of his grandmother, rescued from the Dower House after her death, but this one was his favourite because he could see the fierce, partisan love in her eyes.

She was the only person who had ever truly had his back. Everything he had, he owed to her. And he would do anything to prove to the world that her trust in him had been justified.

His scowl fading, he slammed his laptop shut, got to his feet and wandered over to the window. As he stood and stared, he forgot his anger and frustration and simply marvelled at the beauty and breadth of the view. An open sky, huge frost-tipped firs and a frozen lake that stretched as far as the eye could see.

He'd lived here for nearly ten years, but he still got excited by the scale of everything—and by the snow. Here in the Great White North of Canada the snow was at its whitest and brightest, pure and unsullied.

Unlike his thoughts, which seemed to be a relentless and erotically charged slideshow of images involving Santa's warm, satin-smooth body pressed against his.

Damn it! What was she doing back in his head?

He gritted his teeth as his groin hardened with swift, intense predictability. Only why shouldn't he fantasise about pressing his wife's barely glimpsed body against his? It was going to be the nearest he got to doing so.

His wife!

His lip curled as the words ticked inside his head like an unexploded bomb.

This had been his brilliant idea. And at the time, holed up in the Haensli, with that pack of paparazzi baying in the snow outside and his shareholders holding a gun to his head, marrying Santa had seemed like the best solution.

Expedient and mutually beneficial, in fact.

He frowned. *Yeah, tell that to the ache in my groin.*
Whatever benefits there were to marrying Santa,

they had stopped the moment they'd walked out of the wedding chapel in Las Vegas.

He'd hardly seen his wife since their stand-off at the top of the stairs. She had joined him for a very stilted supper last night and then retired early to *her room*, claiming tiredness. And this morning at breakfast she had treated him to a silence that would have impressed an order of Trappist monks.

As would the vow of celibacy he had unthinkingly but voluntarily signed up for...

Shoulders tensing, he felt a ripple of frustration wash over his skin. Back in Klosters they hadn't actually discussed their sleeping arrangements. In the scheme of things, it hadn't been top of their agenda.

Had he assumed they would sleep together?

Probably.

Had Santa?

Clearly not, he thought sourly.

And that was infuriating too, because she so clearly wanted to—as much as if not more than he did. His breathing stalled, and he remembered that moment on the landing when they were arguing. When it had felt as though it could all start up again...as if they could kiss and keep on kissing—

She had felt it too. He knew she had.

So how could she do that? Get so close to giving in to the pull between them and then claim that *he* was the one who was confused?

He hadn't been confused, but knowing that didn't change the fact that they were going to be stuck with each other for the foreseeable future.

His jaw tightened. After Marina he had sworn he

would never marry. Not that he'd needed to make any kind of vow. To get that close or feel committed enough to someone required a trust in people he no longer had. And yet somehow, despite being neither close nor committed to Santa, he was now her husband.

But only in public. In private, he'd signed up to live like a monk.

Which was why the less time he spent with her the better.

His gaze snagged on something at the edge of the lake. A flash of hot-pink that was as shocking and unexpectedly out of place in the winter wonderland as a flamingo.

He stared hungrily through the glass, his heart beating against his ribs and then he saw her.

Santa.

His eyes narrowed as she pushed off across the frozen surface of the lake and, pulse accelerating, he watched her skate backwards, building up speed and then turning her body into a perfectly executed triple Lutz before landing effortlessly on the ice.

Seriously?

Suddenly his breathing was choppy, as if he were out there on the ice, not Santa. He felt a rush of heat tighten his muscles. It shouldn't have surprised him that she was skating—after all, it was basically her life. It was certainly the only reason she had agreed to marry him. And yet he couldn't quite believe that she could be out there, acting as if nothing had happened, practising her damn jumps when he was in here, struggling to get his head straight.

Suddenly, rather than spend as little time with her

as possible, he found that he very much wanted to get right up in her face.

It took less than ten minutes for him to pull on boots and a jacket and stalk down to where the lake gleamed beneath a pale but determined sun.

As he stopped at the edge of the frozen water, between a pair of shaggy, snow-flecked spruces, Santa did another seamless sequence of jumps and spins, and he found himself torn between admiration at how they seemed to cost her no physical effort whatsoever and continued resentment that she had so easily tuned out the events of the past few days.

And so easily tuned him out too.

A flurry of ice crystals sprayed up in a shimmering arc as she came to a graceful stop. He felt a jolt of surprise as he realised that she wasn't alone on the ice. His housekeeper's young grandsons, Taylor and Ryan, were there too.

He watched the boys skate after her. Within seconds Santa had them playing tag, and they were chasing one another, the boys' laughter and Santa's giggles rising up through the chilled air.

His heart began to pound. He hadn't seen her like this before. As she smiled, she looked young, carefree, happy. It was like watching the sun break through the clouds on the first day of spring, and more than anything he wanted her to turn that smile his way.

And then, just as if she had heard his thoughts, she did turn—but as she saw him her smile stiffened and the corners of her mouth snapped down.

'Louis!'

The two boys skated across the ice, their faces

flushed with excitement and pride. Santa followed them more reluctantly. Her eyes locked with his and he felt something inside him slip sideways as he watched the flare of heat in her glorious glacier-blue eyes.

Dragging his gaze away, he looked down at the two boys. 'Skating's over for today, guys,' he said firmly, speaking over their chorus of protests. 'I want to spend some time with my wife.'

They both watched in silence as the two boys unlaced their boots and headed off in the direction of their grandmother's house, occasionally stopping to throw snowballs at one another. As they disappeared from view, Santa stepped off the ice.

'I thought you might want rescuing. They can be a bit of a handful sometimes,' he offered.

She was staring at him with the cool-eyed hostility of a prisoner of war. 'I do want to be rescued,' she answered tartly. 'But not from Taylor and Ryan.'

His eyes met hers. 'You know, instead of throwing shade at me you could just say thank you,' he said, not bothering to keep the exasperation he was feeling out of his voice. 'If it weren't for me you would have lost your sponsorship. Your future. Your dreams.'

'If it weren't for you,' she retorted, 'I wouldn't have been put in that position in the first place. So before I thank you, perhaps you should think about apologising to me.'

Damn, but she was annoying, he thought, his jaw tensing. Even more annoyingly, he knew she was right.

Picturing the expression on her face when the paparazzi had surrounded her on the steps of the Haensli, he felt his jaw harden. She had looked terrified, like a doe surrounded by a pack of hunting dogs, and he didn't have to dig deep to admit—to himself, at least—that if he was swapped out of her story then it wouldn't have happened.

But it was a long time since he had apologised to anyone for anything. Not so long, though, that he couldn't remember every single word.

His chest grew tight. And not just his own words. He could remember everything his parents had said—and, more importantly, what they hadn't said. In his mother's case that was particularly easy, as she had said nothing at all. He had humbled himself, gone to them expecting...*needing*...comfort and support, and it had all been for nothing. He had lost everything anyway.

And he hated that it still turned him inside out.

Santa was staring at him intently, almost as if she could read his thoughts. Needing to escape her gaze, and defuse the tension gathering in his chest, he said abruptly, 'I didn't mean for any of this to happen, Santa. But we *are* married, and you agreed to that.'

'Only because you didn't give me a chance to think.'

'Oh, right—and you had so many other options,' he snarled.

Her chin jerked up, eyes flaring. 'You were crowding me and I panicked. I thought I was going to lose everything.'

'And you think I don't know what that feels like?' He asked the question before he realised what he was saying...what he might be revealing. 'You're not the only one who had something to lose, Santa. Callière was named after my grandmother. It matters to me as much as skating does to you.'

It was the only thing that really mattered to him any more.

He bit down on his anger, holding on to his temper by a thread. 'I know it isn't going to be easy. But I also know that if we can't find a way to be civilised with each other then it's going to be a whole lot harder.'

Then, before she could reply—before she could quite rightly ask what gave him the right to be so holier-than-thou—he turned and walked towards the house, feeling the burn of her gaze searing into his back.

Santa stared after him in silence. *Civilised?* She almost laughed out loud. Louis Albemarle might be a member of the aristocracy, but he was probably the least civilised person she had ever met. It wasn't just that he said and did such outrageous things…it was that, unlike most people, he refused to be held accountable for them.

So how could he accuse her of making everything harder? He was the one who had feigned sleep on the flight so as not to have to speak to her. And yet, to be fair, he had come up with the only viable solution to their problem. More importantly, she had agreed to it.

Reaching down, she began to unlace her skates.

Of course she had.

It was either marry Louis or risk everything she had worked for her entire life. And it wasn't just about her. Her father and Kate had sacrificed just as much, if not more, re-mortgaging their house and taking staycations long before it had become a thing. Even her little brothers had gone without.

For her.

They had done whatever was necessary without complaint, and those sacrifices weren't going to have been for nothing. She wanted to win. She wanted to make them proud and that meant she'd had to marry Louis.

It was time she accepted that, and not just accepted it. She needed to embrace it as a choice she had made, rather than seeing it as something Louis had foisted upon her. Otherwise she would spend the next year feeling like a victim.

Her fingers stilled against the laces.

Been there. Done that. Got the photo.

And she never wanted to feel like that again—so passive, so powerless. That had been the worst part of what had happened with Nathan. Worse than the names he'd called her. Worse, even, than knowing everyone was talking about her.

Not having a voice. Not having a say in her own life.

She had been helpless, paralysed with shock and shame and hurt. All she had wanted to do was crawl under her duvet and hide.

But she couldn't hide from Louis for a year.

Straightening up, she gazed at the house, her heart thumping. And she didn't want to. She didn't need to.

He might be a duke, but she was a duchess now.

She was his equal. Her needs and wishes were as important as his.

Her shoulders stiffened as she remembered what he'd said about his grandmother. There had been an emotion in his voice she hadn't heard before, and it was obvious that Callière was more than just a business to him.

It was a legacy.

She understood how that worked. Her mother's

dreams had become her dreams, and were all the more important for that.

Perhaps that sense of responsibility was even more true if you were a member of the aristocracy, where your role was to act as a custodian of your family's future.

She felt a pang of surprise that she and Louis actually had something in common, and remorse that she had misjudged him. Clearly they both wanted and needed this marriage to work, and that meant no additional stress, no point-scoring, no spoiling for a fight every time they met.

In other words, a truce.

She glanced at her watch again.

And what better time to inform Louis of her terms than over lunch?

But it was not to be. They had just sat down to eat when Maggie appeared. Bob Arnett was on the phone. There had been an accident at the mine.

Caught between shock and surprise, Santa watched Louis leave the dining room. Back in Klosters, when he'd said all that stuff about the shareholders, she'd thought he was just having a tantrum. That he might be CEO of Callière, but he'd either inherited the position from some family member or been chosen as a poster boy on the basis of his good looks and even better connections.

It hadn't occurred to her that he took his position seriously, or that anyone else might take him seriously either. But there had been a focus and authority in the long lines of his body as he'd crossed the room, and when Maggie reappeared, to make his apologies for not being able to return and join her for lunch, she wondered if she might have underestimated him.

Was he really that bothered?

Did he care that much about the business?

Still pondering those questions later, she made her way downstairs for supper. She had half expected him to be still holed up in his study, but when she reached the dining room he was standing there, gazing through the glass at the distant peaks.

He turned as she walked in, and she felt her pulse twitch as his eyes moved slowly from her face down over her white ruffled top and dark blue jeans and back up to her lips. He had changed too, into dark grey trousers and a cream crew neck jumper that hugged the muscles of his upper body.

She felt a flicker of irritation as he walked towards her. Or maybe it was lust.

He held her gaze, and the sudden intensity in his eyes made her skin sting.

'Sorry about lunch,' he said.

'Don't worry about it.' She smiled stiffly. 'Is everything okay?'

His expression didn't alter, but she sensed something shift beneath his skin like water beneath a frozen pond as he nodded. 'It is now.'

She knew he was talking about the problem from earlier, but something in the way his eyes rested on her face as he spoke made her think it might mean more than that.

'That's good,' she said quickly.

A shiver ran down her spine as he pulled out a chair

for her, and then he was behind her, so close she could feel the heat from his body as she sat down.

Maggie's roast chicken was sublime, its crisp, amber skin and the olive-oil-roasted potatoes offset by dandelion greens and a shallot confit. To follow there was a delicious caramelised honey, vanilla and orange panna cotta that melted in her mouth.

'I think we'll take coffee in the sitting room,' Louis said, pushing back his chair. 'Give Maggie a chance to clear the table.'

Decorated in a muted palette of pale grey and white, the sitting room was a seamless mix of comfort and contemporary style. A fire was burning brightly behind a smoked glass surround and, positioning herself on the edge of one of the huge cream sofas, Santa leaned into its glow as the housekeeper arrived with the coffee.

'If you don't need me for anything else, sir, I'll be heading off,' she said, putting down the tray. 'Have a good evening.'

'Thanks, Maggie. See you tomorrow.'

Santa gazed after the housekeeper. Louis might have his flaws, but he clearly knew how to choose staff. Everyone she had met so far was polite, unobtrusive and exceptionally good at their job.

Her lip pulled into a slight pout. But no doubt choosing top-notch employees was something dukes-in-waiting were trained to do from birth.

'What have I done wrong now?'

Startled, Santa glanced up and found Louis looking at her, his blue eyes resting on her face.

'Nothing…' She hesitated. 'I was just thinking you have a lot of nice people working for you.'

'You seem surprised.'

She felt her skin grow warm as he laughed softly.

'Oh, I get it. You were expecting some entourage of yes-men.' He raised an eyebrow. 'Or maybe yes-women? All rushing around enabling me and encouraging my vices.'

Her cheeks grew warmer as his gaze locked with hers.

'Sorry to disappoint you. *Again*.'

A tingly shiver ran through her body as he flashed her a shadow of a smile.

'But I don't need to be flattered. What I need is people around me I can rely on.'

If she hadn't been looking at him she would have missed the sudden twist to his mouth. But surely as a duke Louis had that anyway? Didn't members of the aristocracy have loyal family retainers?

He was standing by the fire, staring down at the flames, and watching the light play across the stubble stippling his jaw she felt something stir inside her. She had called Louis a boy, but there was nothing boyish about his face. Her gaze dropped to the muscular contours of his chest.

Or his body.

'Tell me something, Santa. I know you think I'm arrogant and feckless and entitled...' he turned, the intentness in his blue eyes accelerating her racing pulse '...but, putting aside all the things you don't like about me, is there anything that you *do* like?'

Whatever she had been expecting him to say, it wasn't that, and her insides tightened, her body responding instantly to his question.

Yes, yes, yes.

His smile. That beautiful symmetrical face. Those glorious summer-sky-blue eyes. His dazzling confidence.

But she wasn't going to let Louis know just how much he affected her. Lifting her chin, she met his gaze. 'You have a nice house.'

He smiled then, one of those devastating, stomach-melting smiles, and suddenly she wished that they were still fighting. It was easier to be around Louis when her anger was acting like a buffer between them.

Only then she remembered what she'd decided earlier and, taking a breath, said quickly, 'And when you're not being arrogant and feckless and entitled, I think you can be compassionate and reasonable. I mean, you could have just left me to face the music on my own at the Haensli. But you didn't.'

She shivered, remembering the moment when the paparazzi had surrounded her…remembering, too, Louis's hand reaching for her.

'I suppose what I'm trying to say is thank you.'

Her heart thudded as he studied her face. 'My pleasure,' he said softly.

Pleasure.

The word rebounded inside her. Staring up at him, she caught the gleam in his eye and felt her stomach flip over. He was a man whose every word, every glance, promised unimaginable pleasures. Even just looking at him made her head swim.

Hoping her face wasn't betraying any of her thoughts, she cleared her throat. 'And I do want to make this work.

And for that to happen we both need to stop picking over the past.'

'Fine by me.'

'Obviously once the honeymoon is over we'll be able to spend more time apart,' she continued, 'but for now I think we should set some ground rules.'

He screwed up his face. 'I've never been a big fan of rules.'

Her fingers twitched against the smooth leather. She'd had this conversation all mapped out, but unfortunately Louis was going off-script. 'But you said you wanted things to be more civilised…'

He took a step towards her and, looking up into his eyes, she felt something hot lick over her skin.

'I think this *thing* between us more or less rules out any chance of you and I being civilised for very long,' he said.

She felt her heartbeat falter. Now the conversation was not just changing up a gear, but going completely off-piste into dangerous territory. 'I—I don't know what you're talking about,' she lied.

'Then you must either be very stupid or very scared. And I know you're not stupid,' he said softly.

Louis watched as Santa jumped to her feet.

'I'm not scared of you.'

'No, you're not,' he said, his gaze shifting from her face to her tightly closed fist. She was clearly angry with him for pointing out the obvious. 'You're scared of how much you want me. But you don't need to be. I feel it too.'

'There is nothing to feel.'

She was shaking her head, but it was the shake in her voice that interested him. And the glitter…the longing in her eyes.

'None of this is real, Louis. We made it up. For the cameras. For Mr Bryson. For your shareholders.'

'And none of them are here.'

Reaching out, he took her hand and pressed it against his chest, against the thundering of his heart.

'But this is real.'

He watched her pupils flare, the black engulfing the blue as he pulled her against the thickness of his erection.

'This is real too. And it's definitely not for my shareholders.'

They stared at one another for endless seconds, faces barely an inch apart, wide-eyed, gazes locked with a simmering intensity that made the blood thicken in his neck.

And then, breathing out unsteadily, she reached up and clasped his face with her hands, pressing a desperate kiss to his mouth.

CHAPTER SEVEN

IT WAS LIKE a dam breaking.

His breath caught, the feel of her lips maddening his senses, and he pulled her against him, wrapping his hand in her hair. Longing rushed through him as he felt her hands curl into the front of his sweater and she pressed her body against his with a desperate, clumsy urgency that made him almost lose his footing.

He'd thought that kissing her would make sense of how he'd been feeling these last few days, but he didn't understand any of this—not her, not himself, not this insane need. All he knew was that he wanted her, and that his whole being was aching for the satisfaction that only she could give him.

'I've been wanting to do this ever since you got into my limo,' he groaned against her mouth. Breathing unsteadily, he kissed her neck, her throat, finding that sensitive spot just behind her ear.

'I wanted you too...'

Her cheeks were flushed, and he thought a man could drown in the glittering blue pools of her eyes. Liquid excitement raced through his body as her fingers wrenched at his sweater, tugging it upwards and over his head, and he felt his skin twitch as she slid her hands over his chest and shoulders, pulling him closer, her mouth finding his, kissing him back, her teeth catching his lower lip, matching his hunger.

Somehow her top came off, joining his trousers on the floor. He breathed out shakily, his groin hardening as she stared up at him, her dark silken hair spilling over her collarbone. She was wearing a simple white cotton bra. No tantalising lace, no teasing mesh, and yet he didn't think he'd ever been more turned on.

And then, eyes dark with passion, she reached behind her back and unhooked her bra, peeling it from her shoulders. Holding his breath, he ran his hands over her body, feeling her shiver beneath his hands as he cupped her breasts.

Her nipples hardened against the soft skin of his palms and, leaning forward, he kissed her abruptly. Then he lowered his mouth to her breast, his lips closing around one swollen nipple, her soft gasp making him hard and hot in all the right places.

Head swimming, he tugged off her jeans, taking her simple white panties with them, and now that she was naked, a primal need to taste her bit deep.

But as he lowered his head she reached out, her unsteady fingers fumbling with his boxers, and then she pulled him free, her hand curling around the hard length of his erection.

The lightness of her touch was almost an agony. He wanted so much more.

For a moment he thought about picking her up and carrying her to his bedroom. But he didn't want to risk a change of pace or derail this head-spinning outpouring of heat and hunger.

And then his thought processes were short-circuited as Santa pushed him back onto the sofa. He sat down and in the space of a heartbeat lifted her in one strong movement onto his lap, breathing hard as she guided him into her body.

Suddenly he was there, inside her.

Her face was soft, her head tipped back, and he felt his self-control snap. Heartbeat raging, he cupped her breasts in his hands, licking first one, then the other, his body iron-hard as she arched into him, almost frantic in her movements.

She was so hot and tight…the feel of her was turning him inside out…

Somewhere nearby his phone buzzed, but frankly it could have burst into flames and he wouldn't have cared. Nothing mattered except the feeling of Santa's flesh against his.

His breathing was ragged now, and he groaned softly. Forcing himself back from an edge he'd never been as close to before, he began to move slowly, surrendering to the sweet bliss of her body gripping his.

And then he felt her tense against him, her body no longer soft and open but still, taut, like an animal sensing danger.

Lifting his face, he stared up at her in confusion, his heartbeat jolting. 'Santa…?'

She didn't reply. Her eyes were wide with shock, and panic, and something else he couldn't name. As if she had woken from a dream.

A bad dream.

'What is it?' he asked hoarsely.

'I'm sorry. I can't do this.'

He was still trying to bridge the gap between her words and her flushed nakedness when she shifted upwards, lifting her weight.

The air felt chill against his skin and he made a noise in his throat. He couldn't help himself. It felt as if she was taking a part of him with her.

'Santa…' he said again. But she was already crouching down, one hand clutching her top in front of her naked body, the other fumbling for her jeans.

Her face was almost unrecognisable from the moment before. Then her eyes had been intent on him— intent with longing. Her cheeks had been flushed with the need and want he knew matched the hunger written all over his face. Now, though, she looked young and lost. And scared.

'I'm sorry.' She was pulling on her top blindly, mechanically. 'I know it's not fair, and I know it's my fault. I shouldn't have kissed you, but I can't do this—'

His brain still struggling to make sense of what was happening, he pushed his erection back into his boxers, his groin twitching in protest. He barely gave it a thought, too distracted by the bruise in Santa's voice and by way she was holding her body as if it was about to fly apart.

She had pulled on her jeans now, and her bra and panties looked small and helpless in her hand.

'It's okay,' he said automatically, his remark pointless and absurd since it so clearly wasn't. Then, even more absurdly, 'I'm not going to hurt you.'

The thought that she believed he might was more

painful than the ache in his groin and he got to his feet, wanting, *needing* to say something to make her understand that. But she was already moving, running lightly across the pale wooden floor in her bare feet, her loose hair whipping after her as she reached the doorway and disappeared into the darkness.

He didn't go after her.

It wasn't that he didn't want to…his legs just wouldn't move.

Dropping down onto the sofa, he stared into the glow of the fire, shivering in the vacuum left by Santa's absence. His skin felt cold and clammy, and a pulse was throbbing in his neck, beating so hard that he couldn't swallow, couldn't breathe.

He had been unprepared for her kiss, but nothing could have prepared him for what had just happened. Although right now he couldn't say for sure what that was.

Breathing out shakily, he replayed the evening inside his head.

There had been a moment when he'd first felt her withdrawal… He'd thought she'd suddenly remembered contraception, and in that moment he'd actually been grateful, because for the first time in his life he'd forgotten about it too. He'd been too caught up in Santa and her satin-smooth skin and her soft mouth, and how her body had moulded into his as if it were made for him.

Remembering her face when she'd shifted off him, he felt his stomach twist. He had never had a woman run away from him before. Normally he had the opposite problem: women thinking that sex would somehow lead to something more serious.

His mouth twisted. *Like marriage.*

Only now he was married to a woman who had literally fled from his embrace.

It didn't make any sense. He had felt her response. She had melted into him. And you couldn't fake that heat, that fire, he thought fiercely.

You couldn't fake fear either.

And she had been scared. He'd seen it in her eyes.

So what had happened?

What had scared her?

His shoulders tensed in a sharp, involuntary spasm. He felt as if he might throw up. His whole body was vibrating with a tension he didn't want to feel, but couldn't seem to override.

Of course, while it might be true that nobody had ever run from him before, he had been rejected—banished, in fact.

His parents had turned their backs on him. Not publicly—that would have simply added to the scandal—but he had been stripped of his allowance and forbidden from going to Waverley.

The one and only time he had visited the estate in the last ten years had been for Glamma's funeral, and he had gone thinking that shared grief might bring about some kind of reconciliation with his parents, hoping that they might talk. But his father had looked right through him as if he weren't even there.

And then he had done the same thing himself, when his mother had called just a week before his father's death. He had heard her voice, and his anger and misery had been so intense that he hadn't been able to breathe, let alone speak. He had hung up. And now his father was gone, and they would never talk again.

In all probability Santa would never talk to him again either. And now, just like then, he was sitting in the darkness alone.

He ran his hand over his face, turning his back on the memories and the vortex of emotion they had momentarily produced, and then, reaching down, he began to pick up his clothes.

His fingers stilled as he spotted a scrap of white cotton. Santa's underwear. She must have dropped them as she fled.

His hand tightened around the soft material as he remembered the moment she had slipped out of them and the heat in her eyes.

So what had happened? Where had it all gone wrong?

He'd been asking himself those same two questions over and over again, but now he realised he'd been asking the wrong thing. What he should have been asking was how could he make it right?

His heart was suddenly beating loudly inside his head, so that thinking was impossible. But it didn't matter. He already knew the answer to that question.

Santa was skating round the frozen lake. Skating in circles round and round, so that the world was just a blur of white. Fleeing from the memory of the night before as she had fled from Louis.

She still had no idea how she had got to her room, but once there she had spent the remainder of the night fully clothed, watching the door, terrified that Louis would knock and demand entrance—or, worse, force his way in.

Not to finish what she had so recklessly started. She hadn't been scared of that…of him. What had kept her rigidly awake had been the fear that he would want answers, an explanation. And she might want to give him one. And she couldn't bear the idea of Louis knowing the truth.

Too miserable to sleep, too strung out to cry, she had waited until it was light enough to see her hand in front of her, and then she had got dressed and come down to the lake.

It wasn't the first time she had skated like this.

When her mother had been killed by a drunk driver she had been having a skating lesson, and Merry's father had come to collect her. She had been only six years old. But when she'd looked up and seen him waiting at the side, she had known something terrible had happened, and so she had skated in circles until finally her coach had taken her hand and led her off the ice.

Inside her jacket, her clothes were damp with sweat, and her legs were aching now, burning as if they were on fire, her chest too, so it was difficult to breathe. But she kept on skating. Round and round the lake. She couldn't stop. If she stopped the pain would start—a different pain…a pain that was all the worse for being self-inflicted.

An image of Louis's beautiful face jumped out at her from the white blur. In some ways the kiss had been the same as last time—the same tidal wave of hunger that had driven out everything but Louis and the fierce, hot press of his mouth and his hands anchoring her body to his.

But in the most obvious of ways it had been nothing like that first kiss, because this time she had kissed him. Still flushed from her pep talk earlier, she had acted on her desire, wanting to master the past, stupidly believing that for some reason her small act of will might produce a different outcome. That it would be different with him.

That she would be different.

And at first it had been different—wonderfully, amazingly different. Louis was nothing like Nathan, and his touch had unleashed a firestorm through her body, obliterating everything but the flex of his hands against her skin and her own quickening breath.

The pain began again and she skated faster.

She had felt different too. Free and uninhibited and powerful. A woman taking and demanding her pleasure.

And then she'd heard it. His phone. It had been there on the table all along. She had known logically that it didn't mean anything, but she hadn't been able to stop the panic swelling in her throat, swamping her.

Suddenly she had seen herself as Nathan had seen her...as Louis would see her. Clumsy and clueless and embarrassing. A let-down.

A disappointment.

Her eyes were burning now, the tears falling freely, and finally she could skate no more. Just like before, she was going to have to come off the ice and face reality.

Face Louis.

After unlacing her skates, her body aching and exhausted, she made her way up to the house.

She still had no idea what to say to him. Ideally, he would be coldly furious. Then she could take refuge in anger, and that would make everything a lot easier.

Most likely, though, he would simply avoid her.

Or maybe he wouldn't, she thought a moment later as she stepped onto the deck behind the house. Louis was waiting for her.

Her heart bumped into her ribs and she gripped the handrail tightly as the solid wood beneath her feet seemed to turn into quicksand.

He looked up, his blue eyes resting on her face. 'You missed breakfast.'

It was neither a question nor an accusation, just a statement of fact, and she felt a rush of relief.

He looked pale and his hair was tousled, as if he had been skating in circles for hours too, and then she realised that he wasn't wearing a jacket—just the jumper he had worn yesterday.

'How long have you been out here?' she asked.

'An hour or so.'

'Without a coat? You must be freezing.'

'Careful,' he said softly. 'You almost sounded like a wife then.'

Their eyes locked, and then he shrugged.

'It's okay. I needed to clear my head. Think through some things.'

He left the sentence hanging between them.

'Right.'

It was all she could manage. She didn't want to ask him what he had been thinking about. She didn't need to. She was pretty sure she already knew, and she certainly didn't need to hear him say it out loud.

But evidently Louis didn't care about any of that.

Getting to his feet, he gestured towards the door. 'I need to defrost, and you need to eat, so let's go inside and we can talk while we do both.'

'I don't want to talk.'

His face was unreadable. 'You don't need to,' he said blandly.

Inside, the house was unusually silent and still. 'Where's Maggie?' she asked, glancing round the empty kitchen.

'I gave her the day off.'

She felt her pulse accelerate as he pushed a plate of croissants across the table.

'Fortunately, she made these before she left and, after extensive training, I can work the beast—' he gestured at the imposing state-of-the-art stainless-steel coffee machine '—so I'll make us both an espresso.'

Santa didn't want coffee and she wasn't hungry. But she was too exhausted to argue, and at least eating gave her something to do while Louis fixed the coffee. Picking up the croissant, she broke off a piece and put it in her mouth. It was delicious, buttery and light, with a hint of caramel sweetness.

'Thank you,' she said stiffly as he held out a coffee cup and sat down opposite her.

There was a long pause while they both drank their coffee, and then Louis put down his cup. 'I know you don't want to talk about what happened and that's fine.'

His mouth—his beautiful curving mouth—twisted into the kind of smile you might give a stranger: polite, careful, finite.

'I think sometimes actions speak louder than words, and last night was one of those occasions.'

Her fingers jerked against her cup, slopping hot liquid into the saucer.

'It's complicated.'

And ugly and shaming, she thought, trying to blank out both the tenderness in her chest and the utterly stupid longing to reach over and touch his face, as if touching him might wipe clean the distance in his eyes and magically turn back time to when he had looked at her last night, so fierce and focused on her.

'I can do complicated,' he said softly.

She stared at him, a tiny bud of hope pushing up through her misery. Could she tell Louis? Could she share her shame?

Of course, you can't, she told herself savagely, her eyes dropping irresistibly to the ring on her finger. He might be her husband, and he might have made vows in front of witnesses, promising to love and cherish her, but theirs was a marriage of convenience.

Louis was staring at her, waiting for her reply, but she didn't nod or shake her head. She couldn't. She was too scared that moving might loosen the tears building in her throat.

For a moment he didn't speak, just kept staring at her, and then he said briskly, 'I know we both wanted it to, but this marriage isn't going to work out. So I think it would be best for both of us to cut our losses and move on.'

She blinked, his words booming inside her head. Her chest hurt. With an actual, physical pain as if he had punched her. 'Move on...what does that mean?'

'Whatever you want it to mean.' His face was a beautiful, blank, impenetrable mask. 'Divorce. Annulment.'
Annulment.

The cup was suddenly a lead weight in her hand.

'Because of last night?' Numb, shaking inside, she stared at him in horror and disbelief.

He nodded. 'Yes, because of last night.'

The room was spinning. 'No...' Her voice was raw with shock. '*No.* I know you're angry, and I understand that, but we can't split up now—not after everything we went through to make this happen.'

She knew she was speaking, but the words jerking out of her mouth sounded misshapen and unfamiliar, almost as if she was a ventriloquist's puppet.

'It's only for a year,' she whispered.

But Louis was shaking his head. 'It's over, Santa.'

'No!' This time her voice was louder. 'It'll look like we made it up.' In other words, it would appear to be exactly what it was. A sham. A lie. A hoax. 'I'll lose everything...' Her hands clenched against the tabletop.

'No, you won't.'

There was a strange light in his eyes. Standing up, he walked over to the coffee machine and picked up a piece of paper and a pen from the kitchen counter.

'Here. I drafted it this morning. I think it pretty much covers all the key points. But, like I say, it's only a draft. If you want to change anything, feel free.'

Silence hung over the kitchen as Santa stared down at the paper. For a moment the print seemed to swim in front of her eyes, as if she had a migraine forming, and then words began to take shape.

She breathed out unsteadily. He couldn't be serious?

'I don't understand…' The paper was shaking in her hands and she let it drop onto the table. 'This isn't what happened. It's not true.'

He shrugged, his eyes fixed on hers. 'It's as true as what we told everyone three days ago.'

Her chest tightened. 'But you're taking all the blame.'

He smiled then, but the expression in his eyes was bleak. 'Won't be the first time. And you don't need to worry about me. I can take care of myself.' Reaching across the table, he took her hands in his. 'This way, you get a Get Out of Jail Free card. You can start over.'

He lifted his hands and, glancing down, she felt her stomach knot. His ring finger was bare, and her eyes burned hot as he placed the golden band on the table-top.

'You'd do this for me?' she said hoarsely.

Now he looked away, staring across the huge kitchen as if he was seeing something more than the stainless-steel range and the clean white units.

'I rushed you…pushed you into this. And it might only be for a year, but I'm not going to hold you to this—lock you into a marriage with a man you don't love or respect or even like.'

'But I—' Santa tried to protest.

Louis cut her off. 'Look, Santa, I know you don't have a very high opinion of me, and that's okay. Most of the time I don't have a very high opinion of myself either.' He sucked in a breath. 'But I want you to know that I would never hurt you, and I'm sorry I scared you last night.'

Her stomach twisted. *No, that was wrong.* This was wrong. Maybe if he hadn't taken that phone call yesterday she might have felt differently, but now she knew he cared about his business. About his staff.

And he was going to lose everything.

Only it wasn't fair for him to be punished for something that wasn't his fault.

She felt her breathing jolt. 'I wasn't scared of you.'

If someone had asked her, she would have said that her brain was a mess, incapable of functioning, and yet the sentence came out fully formed, as if it had been sitting there just waiting to be spoken.

His eyes narrowed on her face. 'You ran away from me, Santa.'

'Not you.' She shook her head, and now that shake was filling her voice. 'It wasn't you,' she said again.

She could feel disbelief radiating from him. 'There was no one else there,' he said, his jaw clenching.

'Yes, there was.'

Blinking back her tears, she pressed her hand against her chest, pushing at the ache of misery, trying to hold everything in. But the words rose up inside her.

'I was there. And that's who I was running away from. Me. The person I am. The person I *really* am.'

Louis stared at her in silence, a pulse throbbing too hard and too fast in his neck. 'I don't understand.'

She was shivering, one hand clenched tightly, the other limp against the table.

'I thought I could do it. I thought it might be different with you—that I could be different. But I'm still her.'

Still who?

He felt his jaw tighten. In the past, if a conversation had become this intensely and bafflingly personal, he would have changed the subject or walked away. But he didn't want to walk away this time. He wanted to do or say whatever it took to make that haunted look on Santa's face go away.

Watching her eyes slide to the door and the stairs beyond, he was suddenly scared that any pause in the conversation might send her spinning away from him like last night, so he said quickly, 'And that's why you ran away?'

'I didn't want it to be like that with you.'

He clenched his teeth, hearing and hating the ache in her voice. Reaching across the table, he unpeeled her hand, and pressed it against his. 'Be like what?' he said gently.

'A disaster.'

The word sounded both stark and ridiculous in the brightly lit kitchen.

'Why would it be?'

She bit her lip. 'Because it was before. With Nathan.'

His jaw tightened, the name triggering some dull, primitive pulse of jealousy. 'He was your boyfriend?'

She nodded. 'At college.' Her eyes dropped to the floor. 'It was hard for me. I never really fitted in. And when I started winning skating competitions the other kids began picking on me—you know, saying I was stuck up and full of myself.'

He tightened his grip on her hand. 'Kids can be cruel.'

'The teachers stopped it if they saw, but mostly I just put up with it, because I was doing something I loved. And then one day Nathan stuck up for me. I couldn't believe it. He was so handsome and popular.'

Looking at her still, tense body, Louis felt the muscles bunch in his arms. He didn't need to hear the end of this story to know that Nathan had been no knight on a white charger.

'You wouldn't understand.' Her eyes were on his face now. 'I'm not like you. I need to be out on the ice for anyone to notice me.'

Not true, he thought, remembering that first time when he had spotted her at the heliport.

But before he could correct her, she said, 'I suppose I was flattered. I never had time for all the things everyone else did, like sleepovers and parties and boyfriends, but that didn't mean I didn't want them.'

Louis's heart squeezed tight. It was part of the human condition, wanting what you couldn't have. Worse still was losing it when you did have it.

'Nathan told me I was beautiful. That he loved me and wanted to have sex with me.' Her mouth trembled. 'I wanted that too. And when I went to Sheffield for the figure skating championships we agreed that Nathan would meet me at the hotel afterwards.' Another pause, this time longer, and then a tired smile pulled at her mouth. 'I got a gold medal, and then I went to the hotel and we had sex. And it was a disaster. *I* was a disaster.'

Watching her draw a steadying breath, Louis felt his gut twist. It was all too easy to imagine Santa as a gauche teenager. An outsider desperate to be accepted, to be loved.

'You don't know that.' The adrenaline pumping round his body was making the room shudder in and out of focus.

'I do. And it wasn't just me. He made sure everyone else knew too.'

Sliding her hands free of his, Santa found her phone. The pain and shame in her eyes made him want to smash things with his bare hands.

'Here. I know I'm not in the photo, but they all knew it was about me.'

Heart thudding, Louis stared at the screen. It was a photo of a medal. A gold medal, gleaming in the glare of the camera flash. A filmy red haze was colouring his gaze, but not enough to obscure the comment underneath or the gleeful number of 'likes'.

'I don't know if it's still on the internet. This is a screenshot. I took it because afterwards when everyone found out, I lost form, I just couldn't skate and I wanted—' her voice faltered '—I needed to remember my priorities.'

Rage boiled inside him. And guilt—a searing guilt that he had put her in the paparazzi's firing line. No wonder she had been so terrified...so desperate to find a solution.

'It was your first time,' he said, his voice rough. 'Everyone's first time is a disaster. I know mine was. I barely lasted five minutes.'

Tears were spilling down her face and he moved swiftly round the table, pulling her into his arms, holding her tightly against him.

'When your phone rang,' she whispered, 'I remembered what he did and I panicked...that's why I ran.'

He pulled her closer, stroking her back, her hair. Of course she had run from him. It would have felt like a trap closing around her. Anyone would have run.

Ten years ago he had run from a loveless marriage.

But right now Santa needed him, and he wasn't going anywhere. He held her against him, his hand moving slowly through her hair, until finally her sobs subsided and, breathing out shakily, she eased back and looked up at him.

'He's a troll, Santa,' he said hoarsely. 'A pathetic, spineless troll. I'd like to kill the bastard.'

Her shaky smile tore at his heart. 'I don't think that would go down well with your shareholders, but thank you anyway.'

'I'm sorry.' He breathed out, shocked. Sorry was supposed to be the hardest word—he'd certainly felt so yesterday. But saying it to Santa felt like the easiest and most natural thing in the world. 'I'm sorry for everything. For putting you in this position. For kissing you—'

'No.' She reached up and pressed her fingers against his lips. 'I don't want an apology for that.' Picking up the statement he'd written, she tore it in half. 'And I don't want this either. We made a deal, and we're in this together.'

She held out his wedding ring and he stared down at her in silence, her words and the determination in her voice tangling something inside him.

'You'd do that for me?' he said slowly.

As she nodded, she slid the ring onto his finger.

Her eyes were a soft, clear blue and, feeling a sudden nonsensical urge to dive into them, he dropped his gaze. Only now he was looking at her mouth, at those beautiful, curving lips…

He looked up sharply and his whole body stilled as he realised she was looking at his mouth. Leaning forward, he let his lips touch hers—a fleeting whisper of contact, an unspoken question passing between them.

A second later he felt her answer as she brushed her mouth against his. 'Are you sure about this?' he asked.

She met his gaze. 'I was always sure about you—it was me that was the problem.'

He saw her confidence falter and, shaking his head, reached up and grazed his fingers against her cheekbone. 'You were never the problem. But if you don't believe me then maybe I need to prove it to you.'

'Now,' she said shakily. 'Prove it to me now.'

Bending his head, he took her mouth softly, his body clenching when she parted her lips. Still gently, he deepened the kiss, intoxicated by the sweet caramel taste of her and the warmth of her body. Wrapping his hand around her waist, he felt a heavy throb of hunger pulse through his veins as her body swayed into his and she began to kiss him back, her breath fast against his skin.

Her fingers slid beneath his top, moving over his skin lightly, clutching at his senses, and he pressed into her body, his groin clenching in sharp demand.

'Not here…' he breathed against her mouth as his hipbone collided with the underside of the counter. He wanted a bed for what he wanted…for what he needed to do with Santa. *'Wait…'*

Pulling out his phone, he tossed it onto the counter, and he felt his body harden to iron as her hands caught his top and she dragged him towards her.

They didn't make it to the bed…

* * *

Kissing him urgently, Santa felt her stomach melt as Louis turned them both, his hands burning through the fabric of her top. And then he was walking her backwards into the living room, the two of them stumbling against chairs and tables.

They fell as one onto the sofa, their mouths fused, limbs entwined. Somehow their clothes came off—pulled, tugged, wrenched, discarded—and they were both naked.

Gazing down at his beautiful hard-muscled body, Santa felt her head swim with hunger. She was aroused, but so was Louis—palpably, fiercely…

Last time beneath her desire there had been a fear. Now that was gone. And there was a thrilling power in seeing him so aroused and knowing that she was the reason that made the last remnants of her nervousness and self-doubt vanish.

His hands were moving over her hips and waist in small, maddening circles, and then he cupped both her breasts, pressing them together, his tongue darting between the nipples.

She moaned softly.

Heat was pulsing through her body, shivers of pleasure darting across her skin, and she felt almost frantic in her movements—frantic for him to caress the part of her body that was clamouring loudest for his touch.

As though sensing her need, he caught her leg, drawing it up to bring her clitoris against the hard length of his erection. Her fingers bit into his biceps, her head falling back. The stimulation was enough to send her over her edge. Everything was out of reach, meaningless, except the spasms of her muscles.

As she cried out he shifted backwards, his dark gaze trained on her face. 'I'll get a condom,' he said hoarsely.

'No—' Her hand grabbed his. 'I'm on the pill.'

His eyes found hers. 'And you don't have to worry. I'm careful— I mean, I take care of myself.'

She felt his hands slide under her bottom and then he was lifting her, sliding inside. Of their own accord, her legs wrapped around his hips, pressing him deeper, and he groaned, his breath hot against her face. Then he was thrusting into her, his body tensing and jerking as she arched upwards, her fingers biting into his back, her whole being ablaze and suspended, both of them reduced to a single frenzy.

CHAPTER EIGHT

BLINKING HER EYES OPEN, Santa stared drowsily into the pale grey light. For a few seconds she was utterly disorientated, her brain sluggishly trying to catch up with her surroundings, and then she sat up with a start.

She was in Louis's bed.

Her pulse twitched, the gold band on her finger catching the light as she pulled the sheets up around her naked body, feeling a warm, intoxicating pleasure spilling over her skin.

She breathed out unsteadily. There was pleasure, but also a lightness—as though a weight had been lifted. And in a way it had. Each time Louis had reached for her, his eyes blazing fiercely with passion and need, she had let go another piece of the cold, slippery shame she'd been carrying for years, until finally there had been nothing.

It had taken several attempts for them to actually make it upstairs. Each time either one or both of them had been too desperate, too in thrall to the insatiable hunger between them, to take more than a few steps.

Not that it had mattered.

Outside the window a few stray snowflakes spun

gently to the ground and, watching their casual, downward descent, she felt a swift, tiny smile tug at the corners of her mouth. Louis had definitely proved his point…although there were still some things that she wanted to try out…

'You're awake.'

The teasing masculine voice jolted her out of her thoughts and she turned, a pulse of excitement darting across her skin as she saw that Louis was standing in the doorway, a couple of coffee mugs in his hands.

Heart bumping against her ribs, Santa watched mutely as he strolled into the room. His hair was flopping across his face and he was dressed ordinarily enough, in loose dark sweatpants and a white vest. But his aristocratic features and easy confidence made him look as if he was modelling loungewear for some glossy magazine shoot.

'I thought you were going to sleep for ever,' he grumbled, dumping the mugs onto a table and dropping down into the bed beside her.

Santa frowned. 'Why? What time is it? Oh, my goodness—' she said, her eyes widening with shock as he twisted his watch round so that she could see the dial. 'Why didn't you wake me?'

He tilted up her chin and kissed her softly. 'I thought you needed to rest. I mean, we didn't get to bed until three…' his blue gaze rested on her mouth '…and it's not as if we did much sleeping.'

She could feel colour creeping across her cheeks. 'Not much, no.'

Getting to this place had seemed unimaginable before yesterday—but now, suddenly, she was sitting here in bed, with Louis sprawled beside her, the marks of their lovemaking still visible on their skin, and it all felt so much more intimate than sex.

But was it?

Or had what happened last night simply been a mutual but momentary connection?

Two people just needing to assert themselves over the vagaries of fate through touch and passion and release?

The thought that yesterday might have been enough for Louis made her feel suddenly off-balance, and she pressed a hand against the mattress to steady herself.

Something must have shown in her face because, glancing down at her, Louis frowned. 'What is it?'

'Nothing.' Her eyes dropped to the muscled contours of his chest. 'I just haven't done this before. The morning-after bit.'

He was staring at her, and she felt suddenly stupid beneath the intentness of his gaze.

'It's a bit late to worry about that now,' he said softly. 'I mean, technically, it's the afternoon.'

'I suppose it is…' She bit her lip.

'Hey.' Reaching forward, he pushed her hair behind her ear. His breathing was suddenly unsteady. 'What happened before, with *him*…' he chewed on the word, his voice fierce '…that isn't happening here. Morning, afternoon, evening—whatever time of day or night—I want you,' he said slowly. His hand moved through her hair, his caress warm, measured, precise. 'But perhaps you need more proof…'

It was another hour before they finally managed to make it out of bed. And then, within seconds, a shared shower turned into passion and the soap was dropped, lost, forgotten.

Finally, they were both dressed.

Watching Santa frown with concentration as she pulled her hair into a ponytail, Louis felt his body tense. There was something touching about the careful, precise way she was twisting her hair. It made her seem young and unsure of herself in a way that got under his skin, so that he felt suddenly heart-poundingly angry with the Nathans of this world. Men who used sex and intimacy to bolster their frail egos.

Not that Santa was weak. But, like a lot of talented young people, she had honed one set of skills and in doing so inadvertently stunted the growth of a whole bunch of others.

And yet she was as dedicated and determined as any CEO.

A shiver wound through him as she leaned forward to pick up her watch and his eyes tracked down the line of her back to the splay of her bottom.

She was also a devastatingly passionate woman— and, truthfully, that was what excited him the most. The fact that the poised, immaculate Santa Somerville everyone saw out on the ice turned to flame at his touch.

He liked knowing that she had these different sides to her…liked it, too, that she found it hard to hide behind a mask. It was refreshing and something of a relief. People were complicated, and often contradictory, and life had taught him not to trust anything or anyone who appeared to be outwardly simple and straight-talking.

His lungs felt suddenly too big for his chest.

Not life. Marina.

'What is it?'

Lifting his head, he found Santa watching him. She looked worried, and he felt something pinch inside him. Women liked him, wanted him, but it had been a long time since anyone had cared about him. He didn't count Nick—although funnily enough he *was* pretty sure that his CMO's nagging was motivated by more than self-interest.

But, like he'd told Santa yesterday, he took care of himself. And, for now, he could take care of Santa too.

His chest tightened. She deserved more—far more than that—but that was all he could give her. All he could ever give her.

'Nothing, I'm just starving,' he answered. He took her hand. 'Let's go and see what's for lunch.'

It was lamb, with a bean purée and spaghetti squash. But, frankly, Santa could have been eating cardboard. She barely registered the delicately flavoured vermouth sauce, or the chocolate praline pinecones that followed the lamb. She was too distracted by their newfound ease with one another.

Her face felt suddenly warm. Obviously, some of that was down to sex. For days now they had both been separately on edge, fighting an attraction neither of them had wanted to feel and, in her case, had been terrified to feel, and now that tension was gone.

Only that wasn't the only reason she was feeling less uptight.

Growing up, she had always been quiet and reserved, but after Nathan she had found it hard to trust people, even harder to trust her own judgement, and what had once been shyness had turned to suspicion.

She had been like a hedgehog, rolling into a prickly ball every time anyone got too close. And she had hated the person she had become but felt powerless to change it.

Until Louis.

Glancing over at him, she felt her pulse quicken. He had been wrong. He hadn't pushed her into marrying him. But he had forced her to face her past, and in facing it she was free to write a different story for herself.

Maybe that was why she was happy…happier than she had felt in a long time.

Picking up her glass, she lifted it to her mouth, using it as a shield to hide a small, swift smile. But she couldn't hide anything from Louis.

'What?' he asked.

He was looking at her intently, his fork halfway to his mouth, his blue eyes searching her face.

'I was just thinking how you're nothing like the person in all those tabloid stories.' She'd started the sentence before her brain had had a chance to catch up with her mouth, and now she floundered to a halt. 'You're different.'

'By "different" I'm guessing you mean even more charming and sexy?' he said softly.

Meeting his eyes, she held her breath. His blue gaze was soft like summer skies, and he was so impossibly, devastatingly handsome it was hard not to simply stare and keep on staring.

She bit her lip, feeling suddenly shy. 'No, actually, I meant nicer.'

'*Nicer?*' he said slowly, spinning out the syllables almost as if he didn't recognise the word. 'I can live with that.'

For a few seconds he stared at her in silence, and then, leaning forward, he kissed her. The softness of his lips worked on her senses, so that suddenly she was deepening the kiss, letting her tongue dance with his...

'Oh, my apologies—'

They broke apart. It was Maggie with the coffee.

'I'll just leave this here,' she said, a small smile tucking up the corners of her mouth. 'Enjoy.'

Louis grinned. 'Thanks, Maggie.'

Santa knew her face was flushed. 'I think she knows...'

He rolled his eyes. 'Of course she knows. That's one of the givens of having household staff—they know everything about you. The good, the bad and the ugly.' Taking her hand, he raised it to his mouth, his lips brushing against the cool gold band. 'Or, in your case, the unbelievably beautiful.' His gaze held hers. 'Maggie's cool. She's just happy we've got over our lovers' tiff.'

Lovers.

The word whispered through her body, heating her blood, and suddenly she was so hot and tight she felt as if she would melt from desire.

The feeling of being so vulnerable to him was the strangest sensation, and it should have scared her. Two years ago, even a week ago, it would have done. And yet now it didn't. She wasn't scared of her hunger or of Louis. On the contrary, she felt a previously unimaginable freedom—as if she was on a giant swing, soaring up to the sky, then swooping back down. Every second was more exhilarating and heart-stoppingly thrilling than the next.

'And are you happy about that?' she asked slowly.

He gave her a long, slow, curling smile. 'I couldn't be happier.'

A little while later she was holding his hands, skating backwards, pulling him across the ice. Louis had played hockey when he'd first moved to Canada, but he was definitely rusty on his skates.

'You're having way too much fun,' he grumbled as, laughing softly, Santa tugged him to his feet for the umpteenth time. 'How come you're not covered in bruises?'

'I wear gel pads.' She gave him a quick, shy smile. 'And falling is a skill like any other.'

His eyes met hers. 'I suppose it is,' he said slowly. 'Is it one of those "it's best not to fight it" situations?'

She nodded. 'Pretty much. Basically, just keep your head up. And try not to fall on your knees or your elbows. Or your tailbone,' she added as Louis reached round to rub the bottom of his back.

Grimacing, he shook his head. 'I'll bear that in mind.'

'It's really just repetition. Practice makes perfect.'

'Yes, it does,' he said softly, his eyes locking with hers.

She wriggled free of his grip. 'Which is why I need to practise. And so do you.'

'Ouch.' He grinned. 'And I thought I was doing okay.'

'Well, you've got the basics all in place,' she said,

biting into her lip and darting out of reach as he tried to snatch her hand. 'So just keep doing what you're doing while I warm up.'

They spent an hour and a half out on the lake. After warming up, Santa practised her routine, and then she taught him a simple spin, some bunny hops and a Waltz jump.

Later, Louis said, 'You know you're a good teacher.'

They were in bed by then. They had scrambled up the stairs, tearing at each other's clothes, driven by the primitive, carnal need that had punctuated the day like a heartbeat, and now they lay close, their bodies satiated, their muscles relaxed.

'I used to give lessons at my rink. Mostly to children...just to help pay the bills.' She shifted around to look up at him. 'Bryson's pay for everything now, but before that it was hard.'

There was a beat of silence. His eyes were steady on her face, and she remembered what he'd said earlier about why she had married him. But she wasn't ashamed for not having been born a duchess.

'It must have been difficult to fit teaching in, what with school and your training.'

She shrugged. 'My whole family had to make sacrifices, so I was happy to help. And I really didn't do that much—not like my dad and Kate. They worked two jobs a lot of the time.'

He was caressing her hip, and as she spoke his hand stilled against the curve of her bottom. 'Is Kate your sister?'

'I don't have a sister. Just two brothers, Robbie and Joe. Kate's my stepmother.'

It had been a long time since she'd talked about her mother's accident, and she had forgotten all those mundane, normalising phrases about death that had once been so familiar. But everything she had gone through with Louis seemed to have stripped away her usual reserve so that she found it surprisingly easy.

'My mum died when I was six. A drunk driver hit her car. My dad met Kate a couple of years later, so she's pretty much raised me.'

Louis was listening intently, watching her face. 'But your mum taught you to skate?'

She nodded. 'She was a competitive skater. She gave up when she got pregnant with me, but she took me to the rink almost as soon as I could walk.'

His hand tightened against her hip. 'I'm sorry, Santa.'

'It's okay.' She smiled stiffly. 'It all happened a long time ago.' For a few seconds she was silent, and then she said, 'It's worse for you.'

'Worse how?'

There was a tension in his voice that hadn't been there before and, glancing up, she saw a muscle pulsing in his jaw. But that was understandable. His loss was recent, and came with so many other issues attached.

'You lost your father only three months ago. And that would be hard enough for anyone, but you didn't just lose a father,' she said carefully. 'Overnight you became Duke, and you had to step up and take charge of the family business.'

'Callière is *my* business.' His smile was like the blade of a knife. 'It has nothing to do with my family. Or with you, for that matter.'

The vehemence in his voice, coming so soon after

the fire and tenderness of their passion, hit her with a jolt. 'I didn't know—'

'Why would you?'

Looking up at him, she felt her pulse stumble. His eyes had frozen over and now his face was hardening, like water turning to ice.

'It's not as if either of us needs to share details about our private lives to get what we want from each other.'

Her heartbeat was filling her head. It didn't make any sense for him to be so cold, so distant, when she could still feel the warmth of his hand against her hip. And yet it made perfect sense, and she knew it shouldn't hurt as much as it did. After all, she had known right from the start that this was a marriage of convenience.

Only just for a moment she had got confused. By the sex, by the intimacy, by that feeling of being so in tune with every shift in his breathing.

But of course that was just a trick of skin and shared sweat. It wasn't real. And if she'd been more experienced she would have known that sex, however incredible, was just about bodies. It didn't mean that she mattered to him as a person.

She didn't. She was, and always would be, just a means to an end, and it was embarrassing to have forgotten that fact.

'I think I'm going to take a bath,' she said, slipping free of his hand.

Blanking her mind to how shatteringly significant it felt to do so, she stood up and walked mechanically to the bathroom. Shivering inside, she closed the door. For a minute or so she just stood there, breathing heavily, and then she walked over to the bath and turned on the taps, staring down at the rushing water, wishing she could follow it down the plughole.

An hour later she was still in the bath, eyes closed, reclining beneath the warm, scented bubbles, when the door opened, sending a ripple of cool air across the room.

She opened her eyes. Louis was standing beside her, fully dressed, his hands shoved deeply in his trouser pockets. He looked tense, unsure of his reception, and for a moment they stared at one another in silence.

'I can go if you want me to,' he said finally.

His voice was taut, as if it cost him to speak, and she stared up at him mutely. He was hurting, and even though he'd pushed her away she couldn't push him away now.

Shaking her head, she said, 'I don't want you to.'

Heart beating out of time, Louis sat down on the edge of the bath. Santa was watching him warily, her blue eyes wide and still, as if he were a tiger that had randomly wandered into the bathroom.

His chest tightened. Given how he'd behaved earlier, he couldn't really blame her.

He had hurt her, and it had been deliberate. He'd needed to stop her talking about his father and his family and feeling cornered, he had lashed out, his anger and fear pushing aside all fairness and restraint.

Of course it had all backfired on him anyway. Feeling her warm body withdraw from his had hurt more than he could have imagined.

But not as much as feeling her retreat from him emotionally.

That pain had been unbearable, and he had known then that he had to do something…say something. He'd understood that he couldn't do what he would ordinarily do and push her away—it just wasn't possible. He didn't fully understand why. Probably there was some kind of equation that would explain it…a law of physics, perhaps. All he knew was that it felt as if Santa and he were joined by an invisible thread.

'Could you pass me that robe?'

He held it out for her, watching as she knotted the belt around her waist. It was his robe, and it was huge on Santa. At least four inches of fabric was pooling on the tiled floor, and the rolled-up sleeves made her hands look tiny.

His pulse stalled. She'd had so much to deal with already in her life. Could he really burden her small shoulders with his problems too?

But not to tell her anything felt wrong, cowardly, and disrespectful to the woman in front of him. She had been honest with him, and now it was his turn to be truthful with her.

'I'm sorry about earlier,' he said as she sat down beside him. 'I don't really talk about my father. He and I…we fell out a few years ago.'

An understatement.

'What did he do?'

What did he do?

Louis stared at her in silence, the shock of her question rendering him not just speechless, but breathless. Nobody had ever asked him that before. They had always assumed that, whatever the situation, he was the one at fault.

For a moment the need to tell her everything—every ugly, gut-wrenching detail—swelled inside him. But he couldn't do it. It was bad enough that he had upended her life. She didn't need to know that she was married to a man whose own parents had disowned him.

He shrugged. 'It's not a secret. I was supposed to get married and…well, I didn't. Only they were more wedded to the idea than I was.'

His smile felt like one of those grimaces on a Halloween pumpkin.

'My father was particularly disappointed in me.'

Another understatement.

'And I was upset by his reaction.'

That made three.

'We argued, and I left. The last time I saw him was at my grandmother's funeral, nearly ten years ago.'

The last time I saw him alive, he thought.

And the guilt and regret that had been an unobtrusive companion for months suddenly clutched at him, so that he had to grip the edge of the bath to steady himself.

'That must have been a difficult day,' she said slowly.

He nodded. 'One of the worst.'

In some ways it had been the worst. He had certainly never felt more alone.

'But even before that we had a sticky relationship. My parents had me late—probably too late. I found him stuffy and autocratic, and he thought I was spoiled and entitled.' Looking down at her, he paused, smiling stiffly. 'If I'd been the spare, I think he would definitely have just written me off, but there was only me so we were stuck with each other.'

Santa hesitated, and then took his hand. 'I'm sorry.'

He shrugged. 'Most of the time I was at boarding school. And when I wasn't at school I stayed in the Dower House with Glamma—my grandmother.'

'Is that the same grandmother the business is named after?'

He nodded. 'She was actually Canadian. This house is built on her family's land. She could have stayed here and married a farmer, but she wanted to go on the stage. And that's what she did. She went to Broadway and became an actress.'

'She sounds amazing.'

'She was.' He bent his head away from the shine in Santa's eyes. 'She was beautiful and smart and tough and I loved her. She always had my back. That's why I named my business after her. To thank her for having faith in me.'

'So how did she end up marrying a duke?'

'She met my grandfather at a polo match. She sat in his seat. Then refused to leave.' His eyes found hers. 'Sound familiar?'

She smiled. 'But it was love at first sight?'

'More like love at first fight. Their marriage was pretty fiery, by all accounts. But, yeah, they loved each other.'

She was quiet a moment, and then she said slowly, 'What about your mother?'

His heartbeat accelerated. Part of him had been waiting for that question, but another part had thought, maybe *hoped*, she wouldn't notice the one person he had failed to mention.

But Santa was an elite athlete. She had spent her whole life noticing every small imperfection because the difference between a gold and a silver medal was in the detail.

And his mother was hardly a detail.

'Oh, I disappointed her too,' he said, making his voice sound light. 'We haven't had a mother-son relationship for a long time.'

Her fingers tightened around his. 'But that doesn't mean it's too late to try.'

He thought back to his father's funeral. The guests in their black clothes. The glossy dark coffin. His mother's face, pale and despairing and lost.

'It's fine,' he lied. 'I've moved on. What's past is past. It's history. It's over.'

'So why are we talking about it?' she said quietly.

'Because you brought it up.' His whole body was quivering like a stretched bow string. 'Only you don't know enough to—'

'I know you're angry with your parents,' she said, suddenly and bluntly, 'and that's why you cut them out of your life.'

He had a swift, sharp-cut vision of a stone fortress, vast and impregnable, and then, just like that, her words smashed into it like a wrecking ball and everything he had held back for so long spilled free.

'I didn't cut them out of my life, Santa. They cut me out of theirs when I refused to marry Marina.'

Stomach twisting, Santa stared up at him. His eyes were locked on hers, blazing.

'And do you know why I refused to marry her? Because I caught her in bed with another man the day before our wedding.'

'I'm so sorry...' she whispered.

'Don't be. I'm not.'

There was a flat, hollowed-out note to his voice.

'I know now that Marina did me a favour. She forced me to accept how the world works—how it can only ever work for people like me and her. She made me understand that I couldn't expect to marry for love...that marriage would always be transactional.'

He gave her a small, precise smile.

'Maybe that's why it was easy for me to marry you. And I'm glad I did. I'm glad I could do that for you, Santa. But when this is over I won't marry again. I'm better off flying solo.'

His words felt like a blow to the stomach.

Quickly, compulsively, needing to smother her pain, she said, 'Why didn't you tell your parents the truth about Marina?'

She felt her breath catch. He hadn't taken his eyes off hers but something in them had changed, and now she could see not just anger but pain.

'I did tell them. My father said that it didn't matter, and that he was surprised by my middle-class notions about marriage and fidelity.' His smile looked like it was made of glass. 'He told me that it was too late to pull out...that the reputation of the Albemarles was more important than my ego. He said the wedding was a good match, and I should just look the other way.'

Reaching out slowly, the way she might with a cornered animal, she put her hand on his arm. She was shocked by his words...more so by the fact that they had been spoken by a parent to his son.

He breathed out shakily. 'I was stunned—I didn't

know what to say. So I agreed to do it…to marry Marina. And then I went to a hotel and started drinking, and I didn't stop until the following evening.'

Her heart felt as if it was about to burst. 'Then what happened?'

'I went home. I knew my father would be angry, but he was beyond angry. He said I'd let him down. Let the family down. I tried to apologise, to explain why I couldn't go through with it, but he wouldn't listen. He told me that I wasn't fit to be Duke and that he wanted me gone. That night. Out of the house. Off the estate.'

She felt as if something jagged was pushing into her chest. 'Oh, Louis, that's awful…'

He gave her a small, taut smile. 'He cut me off financially. I didn't have any income. I didn't have anywhere to live. The press were hounding me. I was exhausted. I kept calling him, leaving messages, but it was like I didn't exist. If it hadn't been for Glamma I don't know what I would have done. She gave me money to live on and the deeds to the land in Yellowknife.'

Santa felt shame rise up inside her. She had believed him to be spoiled and entitled, but the truth was that he had been betrayed by his fiancée and banished by his parents. Parents plural.

'What about your mother?' she asked.

His smile was a swift, wrenching thing. 'Henrietta? She didn't say anything. She just stood there like a statue.'

She felt his fingers tighten around hers.

'After my grandmother died, I changed. I stopped calling my parents and I stopped caring about what people thought. If things got carried away, I just put my hand up for it—I mean, my reputation was shot anyway.'

Santa's stab of pain was so sharp, so vivid, it felt real. 'So that's why you offered to take the blame for what happened in Klosters?'

He nodded. 'And then the business took off, and I just capped the past. Only then one day out of the blue my mother called me.' A muscle flickered in his cheek. 'It was the first time I'd heard her voice in nearly a decade, and it just threw me completely, so I hung up. My father died a couple of days later.'

He looked suddenly exhausted, and without thinking she slid both her arms around him. 'You weren't to know...'

'I just wish I'd spoken to them. To him. Only now it's too late.'

'It's not too late,' she said quietly. 'Not while your mother's alive.'

Louis flinched. It was a reflex response, a tiny involuntary shift in the angle of his shoulders, but her eyes flicked to his and he knew that she'd noticed and that she was holding her breath.

He was too.

But he couldn't hold his breath for ever.

'It would mean going to Waverley.'

He had meant his voice to be expressionless, but he could tell by the way her eyes found his that he'd failed.

'What's Waverley?'

It was everything. Not just a house, but a legacy he had failed to live up to. It was his past and his future. It was the family he'd loved and lost.

His chest tightened. At the time he had been young, and devastated by Marina's infidelity. Now, though, he knew that his pride had been mauled more than his heart, and that what had really cut him to the bone was his parents' rejection.

And, whatever he might have told himself in the intervening ten years, that pain hadn't faded. He'd just been hiding from the truth, holed up here with his past in this beautiful, carefully constructed prison of his own making.

Only now Santa had opened a door and shown him a view that was so beautiful, so brimming with possibilities, it made him breathless.

'Louis…?'

He turned. 'It's the seat of the Duke of Astbury.'

'But *you're* the Duke of Astbury.'

As he nodded, she frowned.

'So who lives there?'

He sucked in a breath. 'Nobody. It's empty. It's been empty since my father died. My mother moved out into the Dower House. But I live here now. I can't go back.'

There was a long silence, and then Santa lifted her chin, something flaring in her eyes. 'Maybe you can't—but *we* can.'

He stared at her, so confused by the fierceness of her voice that for a moment he didn't take in what she was saying. 'That's not going to happen,' he said finally.

'Why not?'

'For starters, there's nowhere for you to skate.'

She was staring at him, her jaw jutting in a wordless challenge, and he wondered when he had seen that expression on her face before. And then he remembered. It had been just before she'd forced him to help her climb out onto the fire escape.

Suddenly he knew that Santa wasn't going to let this go.

Her next sentence proved him right.

'This is my honeymoon. Skating can wait,' she said firmly.

The view that had so excited him moments earlier shimmered in front of him like a mirage. Tempting, but treacherous.

'I just need time...'

She was silent a moment. 'Ten years is a long time.'

He felt something shift inside him tectonically, pushing the past up between them. 'Maybe I need longer.'

'Or maybe you just need to go back to Waverley,' she said quietly. 'Because you might live here, but that doesn't mean it's your home. And maybe it won't ever be your home if you don't fix what was broken.'

Fix what was broken.

She made it sound so easy. But fix it how?

'You need to see your mother...speak to her.' Reaching up, she touched his face lightly. 'Let's go to England, to Waverley, together.'

He stared down at her in silence, his heart feeling too big for his ribcage, his lungs suddenly too small to catch a breath.

'You'd do that for me?'

Her fingers stilled against his cheek. 'We made a deal. We're in this together, remember? You helped me face my past. Let me help you face yours.'

Her words reverberated inside his head.

Face the past? Could he do it?

But it was a rhetorical question.

Ever since his father's death he'd felt as if he was running on empty, and that wasn't going to change unless he stepped up and made it change. Unless he went back to Waverley and finished what he'd started.

He had thought of going back before. But each time something had stopped him. Each time it had been easy to talk himself out of it.

This time, though, it felt different. Doable.

But then this time was different. This time Santa would be by his side, with her chin jutting out and her blue eyes sparking with a fire that would lead him out of the wilderness.

So why not go?

His life was on pause so why not go to Waverley and put the past where it belonged? Say goodbye to the ghosts?

And then, in a year, he would buy out the shareholders, and he and Santa would divorce quietly, and finally he would have everything he'd ever wanted.

CHAPTER NINE

GAZING OUT OF the car window at the familiar English landscape, Santa felt a swift rush of excitement skim over her skin. It was completely illogical—she had been out of the country for no time at all—but it felt like a lifetime since she had boarded the plane at Heathrow on her way to visit Merry.

But so much had happened, she thought, turning to look across the opulent interior of the car to where Louis was staring at the view from his own window.

If somebody had told her when she'd arrived in Zurich that she would meet a handsome stranger and then marry him, she would simply have laughed. But now here she was, returning to England not only married but a duchess.

Her spine stiffened against the smooth leather. Right now, though, she was less concerned with being a duchess and more concerned about what the Tenth Duke of Astbury was thinking and feeling.

She eyed Louis sideways.

Outwardly, nothing had changed since their conversation in the bathroom. And if her body hadn't been so closely attuned to his she might have believed that nothing had changed in reality.

But they had spent so much time together over the past week that where Louis was concerned she was like a barometer. Every breath, every word, every glance seemed to resonate inside her, and she knew that he was playing a part.

It shouldn't be such a surprise. They were both of them acting out a marriage for—among others—his shareholders, her sponsor and the world's media. But this was different. He was playing a part for her. And she hated that. But most of all she hated that life had forced him to be so good at hiding his feelings.

Her chest tightened as she remembered the statement he'd written for the press. Even now she was shocked that he had been willing to do that for her. *Won't be the first time*, he'd said. How many other times had he taken the blame for something he hadn't done? And each time another layer of distrust and despair had hardened around his heart.

She felt the car slow and her pulse accelerated. 'Are we here?'

There was no sign of any gates—just a turning into what looked like a smaller road.

Louis nodded. 'We're going to use the tradesman's entrance. I hope you don't mind, but I'm trying to keep everything low-key.'

He sounded calm and relaxed, but she could see the fine lines of tension around his blue eyes and, smiling up at him, she gave his hand a quick squeeze. 'Of course.'

He had magicked up another private jet, and his

household staff had been warned not to discuss their visit. She hadn't even told her family she was coming back to England. She hated doing that, but right now Louis came first.

'Oh, look at the deer.' Leaning forward, she gasped with delight as a herd of fallow deer stopped grazing and lifted their heads with graceful synchronicity. 'Are they yours?'

There was a brief pause and then he nodded. 'There's about three hundred and fifty of them.'

She wondered how he knew. Surely it was impossible to judge that simply by looking.

As if reading her mind, he glanced over at her and smiled. 'Rogers manages the day-to-day running of the estate. He's been keeping me up to speed.'

'What is there to manage?' she asked after a moment.

His lashes flickered. 'The deer, for starters. Then we have tenant farmers, as well as our own herds of sheep and cattle, and obviously with an estate this big there's a constant ongoing maintenance programme.'

She was about to ask him how big—but then the road curved upwards and she saw the house. The sun was low, but even without its rays the pale yellow stone gleamed in the fast-fading light.

'Oh, my goodness…'

She leaned forward again, her mouth dropping open. Her body clock was warped from the switch in time zones, but nothing could detract from the beauty of the huge golden house crouching in the soft green Gloucestershire landscape.

'It's not considered the best aspect. Almost all the

paintings of the house are from the east. But personally I prefer this view.'

'How does it feel to be back?' she asked quietly.

His hesitation was so brief it was barely perceptible. 'Like I never left.'

Maggie's English equivalent, a smartly dressed dark-haired woman named Sylvia, greeted them as they walked into the house, and after Santa had been introduced Louis ordered tea to be brought to their rooms, refusing the housekeeper's offer to accompany them.

'Thanks, Sylvia. I think I can still find my way,' he said, with a tilt of his dark head.

If the house had been impressive from the outside, inside it was even more so. The painted ceiling in the entrance hall had to be at least fifty feet high, and there was a life-size bronze statue of a woman holding a bow and arrow.

Santa glanced across at the two huge, elaborately decorated Christmas trees that stood like sentinels on either side of the staircase. In contrast to Palmer's Point, Christmas here wasn't minimalist, but gloriously traditional.

Her pulse accelerated. In Canada, she hadn't really understood how Louis could live in that beautiful, light-filled house and not see it as his home. Now she understood.

Being here at Waverley, seeing all this and knowing that it had been in his family for four hundred years, suddenly made everything click into place.

As they walked up the huge, imposing staircase, Santa felt Louis's hand tighten around hers. She glanced up at the paintings on the wall, looking for something to say that might distract him a little. 'Are these your relations?'

He nodded. 'That one there is the First Duke, and then they follow in order, right up to the Ninth Duke.' His broad shoulders tensed as they stopped in front of a portrait of a man in a dark suit. 'My father. Edward Albemarle.'

Gazing eagerly at the picture, Santa felt her heart punch against her ribs. She had assumed—wrongly— that Louis would have inherited his father's looks just as he had inherited his title. But where Louis was dark and lean, his father was fair, and although he was handsome, in a kind of plump-skinned, well-fed sort of way, his looks were marred by the imperious expression on his face.

Next to her, Louis was silent.

'You have his eyes,' she said finally.

'Luckily. Otherwise he would probably have doubted his paternity.'

He smiled, but she could feel the effort it took for him to do so.

Glancing down at her, he slid a hand under her chin and frowned. 'You look tired. Come on, you can gawp at my ancestors later. Let's go to our rooms and you can have a lie-down.'

She would actually love to lie down. She had slept on the flight over, but woken half a dozen times, and each time she had been aware of Louis, staring out of the window at the dark night sky.

As he pushed open a door he turned and gave her a small, stiff smile. 'Just say if you don't like it. There are another forty sets of rooms, so it's not a problem.'

She nodded mutely. What was there not to like?

The bedroom was huge—and beautiful. She was going to run out of superlatives very soon, she thought, gazing from the vast oak four-poster bed with its lambent Chinoiserie curtains to the view through the window of a sloping lawn, an endless swathe of every possible shade of green.

'Oh, wow...' she whispered.

'You see that line of trees?'

Louis was behind her, the heat of his body warming her skin. She looked to where he was pointing. It took her a moment to find the trees. They were so far away they might easily be in the next county.

'That is the end of our land.'

Our land.

The words, with their implication of something shared, made her throat contract. But of course Louis had been talking about the Albemarle family when he'd said 'our'.

'I'd love to take a look round.'

He nodded. 'Tomorrow. It's going to be dark soon, and besides, you need to rest.' Taking her hand, he led her to the bed.

He drew back the covers and she sat down and toed off her shoes. 'Are you going to join me?'

He hesitated and then, lifting a hand, he stroked her hair away from her face. 'I think that would defeat the purpose of you lying down,' he said softly, and she felt heat flare in her pelvis as he tilted her face up to his and brushed his lips against hers.

As she lay down, a wave of tiredness swept over her. 'What are you going to do?' she asked.

But before she could hear his reply her eyelids closed and she fell instantly and deeply asleep.

Staring down at Santa, Louis felt his shoulders tighten as her question echoed inside his head.

What was *he going to do?*

Breathing out unsteadily, he walked across the room and stopped in front of the window, his eyes narrowing. A better question would be when was he going to do it?

Back in Canada, he had hugged the thought of returning to Waverley close, like a long-lost toy. Now he was here, though, he didn't know where to start.

At the beginning, maybe.

His heart skipped a beat as he remembered that terrible conversation in the book-lined study downstairs. He had been wholly unprepared for the outcome, and devastated, and yet even now he couldn't regret it. Regret simply wasn't an option for something that had seemed so instinctive and necessary for his survival.

But it had torn his life apart.

From that day onwards every single assumption he'd made about his future had changed. And afterwards he had been too shocked, too numb, to do more than put one foot in front of the other and keep walking, hoping that if he kept walking he could leave the past behind, driven onwards by a need to prove his father wrong.

And not just prove him wrong. He'd wanted to rub his success in his father's face—show him that he didn't need what had been taken from him to prosper.

And he'd done that.

Callière was a global brand—albeit one he currently didn't fully own—and for a time he'd convinced himself that was enough. But it hadn't been. There had always been a shadow behind his heartbeat.

And now he had come full circle. The past he had tried so hard to outrun had pulled him back across the Atlantic Ocean.

His gaze locked on to the tiled roof of the Dower House. Here he was in his childhood home, his mother just a stone's throw away, and finally he could put the past to rest.

At some point he would meet with his mother.

He just needed to find the right time…

But first he needed to decompress.

Reaching into one of his bags, he pulled out their wedding certificate. Heart beating, he unfolded it. He still couldn't quite believe that he was a married man, and yet there it was in black and white.

His eyes snagged on Santa's full name: *Santina.*

At the ceremony he'd been too churned up with anger and resentment to do more than parrot his responses, but now he wondered where that name had come from. He would have wondered more if he hadn't spotted something else—something that made his heart beat faster.

Apparently, it wasn't just Christmas they would be celebrating…

The next day the sun shone with unseasonal brilliance, and they spent the morning driving around the estate. Maybe if he'd been alone the experience would have been different, more conflicted, but having Santa there made it easy for him to just sit back in the worn four-wheel-drive and point out various landmarks on the estate.

He knew she was enjoying herself, but he could also

sense that she was a little surprised that he was giving her a guided tour rather than going to see his mother. Every now and then he would feel her gaze on his face, and each time he felt something inside him crack open.

His spine stiffened against the worn leather. It was ridiculous. He had travelled four thousand miles to be here, and yet he couldn't take those last few steps.

'What's that?'

Gratefully he snapped off his train of thought and glanced over to where Santa was pointing.

'It's my grandfather's folly.' He gazed up at the octagonal Gothic tower that rose beyond the manicured lawns like a bizarrely distorted inland lighthouse. 'He built it for Glamma for their thirtieth wedding anniversary.'

Santa smiled over at him. 'That's so romantic. It reminds me of the Lady of Shalott.'

Her cheeks were flushed, her skin translucent in the pale English sunlight, and with her hair lifting in the breeze she looked more like some farmer's daughter than an international ice skater.

'Doesn't she die on a boat?' he asked.

She laughed. 'I meant the bit before that.'

He liked hearing her laugh, and knowing that he could make her laugh. Liked, too, the pale curve of her throat—more specifically the times it curved for other purposes. Feeling his body harden, he changed down a gear so as not to give himself away.

'My bad. I read it at prep school, so I think I might have skimmed over that to get to the part with Lancelot.' He glanced at his watch and frowned. 'We should probably be getting back for lunch.'

The morning had gone so fast. Too fast. He liked it best when it was just the two of them.

'Oh, look at that house.'

Santa was leaning forward, her eyes sparkling, and he felt something loosen inside his chest as she turned to him.

'It's the Dower House. Isn't that where your mother lives? Why don't we drop in? Louis?' she prompted.

But he didn't answer. The front door of the house had opened, and panic swelled in his throat as a woman stepped into the sunlight. He caught a glimpse of his mother's beautiful face, pale with shock, and then he put his foot down on the accelerator.

'What are you doing?' Santa was looking at him, her eyes wide and confused. 'Why didn't you stop?'

'Just leave it, Santa, okay?' he snapped, relieved to have found an outlet for the emotions churning in his chest.

Her face stiffened and there was a tiny, fractured pause. Then she turned away.

They didn't speak for the rest of the journey.

Almost before he'd stopped the car Santa wrenched open the door and she was gone, moving so quickly that he had to lengthen his stride to keep up with her.

'Santa—'

His anger had burned away and now he felt exhausted and unsteady. The last time she had run from him he had been worried that it might be his fault. This time he knew it was. He had never felt more lonely or alone.

'Santa, please...'

He caught up with her in their bedroom, spinning her round to face him.

'I'm sorry. I didn't mean to bite your head off.'

She stood in front of him, her chest rising and falling. 'I don't understand. I thought you came here to see your mother.'

'I did.'

'So why didn't you stop?'

There was a beat or three of silence and then he breathed out unevenly. 'Because I didn't tell her I was coming. Because I didn't know what to say.'

Santa felt her stomach knot. His skin was stretched tightly over his cheekbones and there was a tension in his body as if he was shouldering an invisible burden.

'I was scared of what she would say. Or even if she'd want to speak to me.'

She caught his arms. 'She called you that time.'

'And I hung up. She reached out to me and I let her down.' He stared past her. 'All these years I've told myself I didn't care. I told myself there was nothing for me here. But now I'm scared that there really isn't anything left, that there isn't anyone left for me.'

'You have me.'

They weren't just words. She meant it. Every waking thought she had was about Louis. She even dreamt about him. In his arms, everything else ceased to matter. Just looking at him stole the breath from her lungs. He had her body, her heart...

Her heart? She felt dizzy. Her pulse was pounding in her head.

It couldn't be true. Theirs was a marriage of convenience. But knowing that hadn't stopped her from falling in love with him.

In love.

The idea was ludicrous—she couldn't be.

But she was.

Somewhere between getting into his limo and now love had slipped into her heart like a key in a well-oiled lock.

She felt a rush of pure, undiluted joy, clear and bright, like the sun reflecting off snow, and she wanted to share it with him as she had shared everything else.

Only she couldn't do that. He hadn't signed up for love. He wasn't looking for 'for ever'. He had told her himself that he would never marry for love and that he would be better off flying solo.

But didn't he only feel like that because of what had happened with his parents? Surely if he and his mother reconnected then he would feel differently about love?

About her.

She could feel his pulse jerking against her fingertips and she tightened her hands around his wrists. 'I know you're scared about seeing your mother, I would be too, but whatever happens you have me. I'll be there with you when you see her.'

The muscles in his arms were trembling. 'You're a good person, Santa,' he said softly. 'Maybe that's why you're the only person I can't lie to. You make me do the right thing.'

'You're a good person too.' Blanking her mind to the riot of emotions pounding through her body, she reached up and clasped his face, pressed a gentle kiss to his lips. 'And I will be here for as long as you need me.'

He smiled then—one of those devastating smiles that felt like winter sun on her face—and then his hands stole around her waist to touch the bare skin of her neck. Stomach melting, she leaned into him, her hands looping over his shoulders.

'I need you now,' he murmured against her mouth.

His hands tightened around her waist and he picked her up and carried her to the bed. He stripped off his clothes, then hers, his sharp intake of breath telling her more clearly than words how badly he wanted her.

Instantly her own body responded, the hunger that he had unlocked rising up inside like a wave. She pressed closer, brushing her nipples against his chest, her breath quickening as he kissed her shoulder, then the pulse beating at her throat, his lips trailing a path lower still to the taut, swollen tips.

Her fingers slid down to capture his arms. She felt wild with need, her body unravelling against his, and helplessly she arched against him, squeezing her thighs together around the ache that was building there.

She felt his hand move, his wrist warm against her thigh as his fingers slid between her legs, slipping smoothly into the hot, slick flesh, his thumb grazing her clitoris so that the ache was just on the right side of painful.

'Louis...' His name was a noise in her throat.

Clutching his biceps, she raised her hips, oscillating her body against the pad of his thumb. She was so close to losing control... Another second and she would be lost, it would be over, and she wanted to hold on to this feeling for as long as she could.

She batted his hand away and, reaching down to where his erection was pushing into the mattress, took him in her hand.

Louis grunted, his body tensing as he felt her fingers slide over the smooth, blood-hardened skin, her touch bringing him instantly to the point where it wasn't enough. He wanted more. He wanted all she had to give.

Only it was more than wanting. What he felt for Santa was need, raw and unfiltered by ego or etiquette.

He couldn't wait a moment longer. He had to have her now.

Shifting slightly, he rolled her over, pulling her body on top of his, blood roaring in his ears as she helped guide him inside her. Her thighs were trembling slightly and, gripping her hips to steady her, he began to move, thrusting upwards into her.

'Yes…' she whispered, and then she tensed.

He felt a tremor run through the fine bones of her body, the muscles clenching, and suddenly it was too late, and his mouth covered hers, and he was grasping her wrists, their hot breath mingling as her cry mixed with his groan of release.

Later, as she lay wrapped in his arms, he felt her shift against him.

'I meant what I said about being there with you,' she said.

Her blue eyes were focused on his face, soft but steady, and he felt something ignite beneath his skin as she put a hand to his chest.

'I know.' He hesitated. 'But what if it's too late? Too broken? I'm not sure I know how to fix it.'

'You do. I know that you think you're not up to it. But the truth is your life—everyone you lost, everything you had taken away, everything you've built— has taught you all you need to know.'

She sat up, not bothering to hide her body, and that confidence, that change from the gauche girl who had been ashamed of herself to this beautiful proud woman, made his heart want to beat its way out of his chest.

'You fix your eyes on the prize and you focus, and then you push forward, and you keep pushing forward.'

He breathed out unsteadily. 'I'd like to go now. If you'll come with me?'

She nodded, her smile as soft as her eyes were bright. 'You should have looked at our marriage certificate more closely—then you wouldn't need to ask that.'

'What do you mean?'

'My middle name is Ruth.' Lifting his hand, she threaded her fingers through his. *'"Where you go, I go."'*

CHAPTER TEN

IT TOOK FIFTEEN minutes to walk to the Dower House. Louis kept wishing they could stop and turn back, but Santa's grip never faltered. Finally they reached the smartly painted gate, and then they were standing by the front door.

'Give her a chance,' Santa said quietly. 'Give yourself the chance to be her son again.'

As the door opened, he felt his heart slip sideways.

'Louis.'

His mother was clutching her throat. For a few quivering moments there was nothing but the blood beating in his ears, and then she was pulling him forward, her hands fluttering over his face, tears spilling down her cheeks.

'I'm sorry… I'm so sorry, darling.'

'I'm sorry too. But it doesn't matter any more,' he said hoarsely.

Inside the house, his mother regained her poise and led them into the light, spacious sitting room. He and Santa sat down close to one another on one of the chintz-covered sofas. Her hand was warm and firm in his.

'Did that come from the main house?' he asked, looking across the room at a beautiful mahogany escritoire. He was only asking because he needed to get his voice under control. He knew it did—only how? Why did he remember so much, and in such detail? It was as if he had never gone away...

But then, of course, a part of him hadn't, he thought, looking up into the familiar brown eyes of the woman sitting opposite him.

'You don't mind, do you?' she asked.

He shook his head. 'It's yours, Mama.' The word slipped from his mouth without hesitation, as if it had been waiting there, primed and ready. But he knew that it hadn't. It had been trapped inside him, stifled by the past, and if it had been down to him alone it would have stayed there unspoken for ever.

But Santa had set him free. She had brought him home.

'There's someone I want you to meet...' He turned to Santa, wanting to share this moment with her. 'Santa, this is my mother—Henrietta, the Dowager Duchess of Astbury. Mama, this is Santa, my wife. The Duchess of Astbury.'

He watched his mother reach out and take Santa's hand.

'Thank you for bringing my son home.'

'He was already on his way, Your Grace. He just lost track of time.'

His mother's mouth trembled. 'We both did.' She smiled shakily. 'I wonder, would you like some tea?'

Santa's eyes met his, and he felt her squeeze his

hand. After a moment he squeezed it back as she shook her head.

'No, thank you. I need to call my father, and you two have a lot of catching up to do, but I hope to see you again soon.'

'I hope so too.'

At the door, he pulled her close, his mouth seeking hers.

'I can stay,' she whispered.

'No, you're right. We have a lot of catching up to do. But I'll see you back at the house.'

Walking back into the sitting room, he hesitated a moment, and then sat down next to his mother. 'I'm so sorry for hanging up on you.'

'It doesn't matter, darling.'

He shook his head. 'He was right. I let you down.'

Her fingers gripped his arm. 'He regretted it, Louis. What he said…how he acted. He regretted all of it until the day he died. But he was such a proud man—and he thought you would come back, that you would need him…us.'

'I did.' His chest tightened as he remembered the nights when he would barely sleep from missing his home, his family. The loneliness had been like a painful head-to-toe tingling. 'At Glamma's funeral I tried to talk to him, but—'

'I know.' His mother nodded sadly. 'Losing her and you so close together knocked him for six. He had a mini-stroke and then he changed, became anxious. I couldn't leave him even for a moment. But I should have tried.'

Her eyes met his. They were surrounded by fine lines now, but they were brighter than ever with love.

'I should have stood up for you,' she said. 'I knew Marina wasn't right for you, even before we found out about that polo player.'

He waited for the sting of pain. But he realised with shock that he didn't care. Marina's betrayal felt like a fly brushing against his skin.

A flash of pink fluttered at the edge of his vision and he glanced out of the window, expecting to see Santa, her body arcing in the snow, her blue eyes fixed on the prize, the flawless facets of her face diamond-sharp, impossible to erase.

But it was just a camelia that was defiantly blooming by the gate.

'Why did you think she wasn't right for me?' he asked, frowning up at his mother.

'Because you didn't love her,' she said simply. 'You thought you did because you're like me—romantic. Your heart rules your head every time. But you're also stubborn, like your father, so that you can't see what's right in front of your nose.'

The next day Santa woke late, and for the first time in days she found herself alone. The curtains were still drawn and she sat up, feeling a rush of panic. And then she heard the sound of running water from the bathroom.

It was okay… Louis was just taking a shower.

Pressing her hand against the imprint in the mattress, where the sheet was still warm from his body, she lay back down and stared into the grainy half-light, trying to absorb the detail amid the wider pattern as the events of yesterday swirled inside her head like a carousel.

One particular detail to be precise.

She bit into her lip. How had it happened? How could she have been so stupid as to let herself fall in love with him?

Shivering, she pulled the covers over her body.

More importantly, how was she going to cope when he was no longer in her life? And that day *would* happen—because this arrangement was temporary. A year-long, mutually convenient sticking plaster over the mess they had made in Klosters.

Yes, they had moved the boundaries. Now sex was part of that arrangement. But no matter how passionate or tender, it was still just sex. And that only made her heart ache more.

'Good morning.'

Louis was standing in the doorway, a towel wrapped around his waist, his dark hair damp, droplets of water glistening like diamonds on the smooth, tanned skin of his formidable chest.

'And it's not just a good morning, is it?' he said softly, walking towards the bed. 'It's a very important one.'

Pulse accelerating, she stared up at him mutely. Her heart might be breaking but her body still reacted to his nearness with unfiltered intensity, so that it was all she could do not to reach up and pluck the towel free of his waist.

He leaned forward and kissed her on the mouth. 'Happy Birthday, Santa baby.'

She blinked up at him. With everything that had been

happening, she had lost track of the days. But today was Christmas Eve, and therefore today was her birthday.

'Come with me. I have a surprise.'

Taking her hand, he led her across the room to the window and pulled back the curtains. Outside, the world had turned white.

'It snowed!' She turned to him, her lips curving into a smile. She felt suddenly and inexplicably happy. 'I can't remember the last time it snowed on my birthday. Can we build a snowman?'

In the bleached sunlight, his eyes were very blue. 'As long as you promise not to wear four-inch heels.'

Remembering that early-morning walk through the silent snow-covered roads, his jacket around her shoulders, his hand tight around hers, Santa felt her heart tumble. But just because her feelings had altered, it didn't mean she could alter the past and make it more than it was. He had simply kept her from falling...got her safely home.

'How did you know it was my birthday?'

'The marriage certificate. And I double-checked with your passport.' He grinned. 'Cute photo, by the way.'

She punched him on the arm. 'It was a mistake. I went to a different hair salon and I don't think they understood what I wanted. Besides, no one looks good in their passport photo.'

'*I* do.'

He started to laugh, and then Santa was laughing too, and he pulled her against him, folding her into his body.

'So—I thought we'd have a birthday brunch, and then you get to choose what we do this afternoon.'

She glanced over at the clock. 'What do you suggest we do between now and brunch?'

'Well, I know Sylvia has planned a feast…' His eyes were steady on hers and she felt heat dart beneath her skin like a shoal of tiny fish. 'So I thought it might be a good idea to work up an appetite…'

Two hours later they made it downstairs.

'Don't you want to go and look at the snow?' he asked.

She felt a quick head-rush as he tilted up her face and kissed her on the mouth, his fingers curling into the belt loops of her jeans to pull her closer. His eyes were a glittering, sapphire-blue, and there was an expression in them she couldn't fathom.

Probably he was just fired up with relief at having finally made peace with his mother. Or maybe he was excited about the snow. Robbie and Joe were the same and so was her dad, now she came to think of it.

'Yes, of course I do.'

'You first.'

He nudged her forward and she opened the door, her body tensing with anticipation at the pleasure of the first crunching footstep.

She froze.

A twisting path of rose petals in every shade of pink led away from the house, cutting a brilliant line of colour across the flawless white.

She let out her breath in a little flurry and caught it again. Her heart was galloping like a thoroughbred inside her chest. 'What…? Where does it go?'

He seemed pleased by her reaction. 'Let's find out,' he said softly, taking her hand.

Feeling as if she was walking on air, she followed the trail of petals across the lawn, past the snow-laden topiary hedges of the formal garden—and then she knew where they were going.

The door to the tower was open. Inside, the petals continued up the winding staircase to another door and another smaller staircase. Her fingers tightened around his as she reached the top step.

'Happy Birthday,' Louis said quietly.

Santa pressed her hand to her mouth. Not that there were words for what she was feeling. Nor could she have spoken them anyway.

It was a tiny chocolate box of a room.

There were windows on all eight sides, each with a view of the pristine white landscape. The walls were decorated in a pale raspberry silk, and beneath the tiny, glittering chandelier a log fire glowed orange.

A huge picnic hamper sat on a table by one of the windows, and taking up the rest of the space was a beautiful glossy mahogany sleigh bed, complete with snow-white bed linen.

Trembling inside, she turned to face Louis. 'You did this for me?'

'I wanted to surprise you.'

'Well, you have.'

'Good.' He smiled—one of those dazzling, impossible-to-resist smiles. 'But, much as I'd like to take all the credit, my part was largely limited to making a whole lot of unreasonable demands at impossibly short notice. My long-suffering staff did all the hard work.' His hand slid among the strands of her hair.

'They'll probably all give notice later, so you might have to help me cook the turkey tomorrow.'

He was trying to downplay it, but it had been his idea. He had made it all happen. *For her.*

Her eyes sought his. Hoping, longing to see what was in his heart. But his eyes were a familiar teasing blue and, deciding to focus on what his actions meant rather than on what they didn't mean, she smiled.

'I'll make sure I thank them. But thank you too, Louis.' She kissed him softly on the mouth. 'It's the loveliest surprise I've ever had.' She leaned into him. 'I'm starving. Can we look inside the hamper? Or have you not worked up enough of an appetite yet?'

His body stilled, his eyes sliding towards the bed, then back to her face.

'Now that you've said you're starving, I suppose we'll have to look inside the hamper,' he grumbled, as she took his hand and led him across the room.

They ate by the window, gazing out across the wintry fields.

'My picnics are a little more basic than this,' Santa confessed, as Louis handed her a glass of chilled champagne.

And by 'basic' she meant supermarket baguettes with clumsily cut cheese in the middle, a bag of crisps, a chocolate bar and a piece of fruit washed down with tea from a Thermos.

'My father was a big fan of *al fresco* eating,' Louis said, forking some of the smoked ham hock salad into his mouth. 'He thought it was the truest test of a great country house kitchen. How's the gravadlax?'

'It's delicious.' She glanced down at the jewel-pink

slices of salmon with their delicate herb crust. 'So, did you go on lots of picnics when you were little?'

Louis hesitated, his fork in mid-air, as if her question had caught him off guard. 'Yes, we did,' he said finally. 'We used to go down to the lake and row out onto the island. Sometimes we'd get up early and my father would take me out fishing.'

She looked up at him, enchanted by the softness in his voice and by this new openness between them.

She frowned. A phone was ringing. Hers. She glanced down at the screen. 'Sorry... It's my dad, video calling. I don't have to speak to him now. I can take it later.'

He shook his head. 'It's your father. Of course you should speak to him now.'

Clumsily, she swiped upwards. There was a short pause and then she started to smile, as an enthusiastic rendition of 'Happy Birthday to You' spilled into the room.

'Thank you—that was brilliant.'

'We didn't wake you, did we?' Kate looked at her anxiously. 'We thought you'd be up anyway...you know, to train...but then we worried that you might be having a lie-in.'

'Kate was worried.' Her father grinned. 'I knew you'd be up.'

'I'm actually having brunch...' She glanced over at Louis.

It's fine, he mouthed.

'Hey, there!' Shifting forward, he waved lazily at the screen. 'We thought we'd make the most of the day as it gets dark so early.'

Santa felt her heart twist as one of her brothers leaned forward. 'Do you have a crown?' he asked.

Grinning, Louis shook his head. 'I don't, sadly. But there is the Astbury tiara, which is a kind of crown, and as Duchess your sister gets to wear that.'

Both boys leaned closer to the screen. 'Can we see it?'

Louis laughed. 'Sure, just not right now.'

Instantly the boys refocused on Santa. 'Have you opened your presents yet?'

'Can we see them?'

'Robbie, Joe—that's enough.' Frowning apologetically, Kate pulled them back. 'Sorry, they're just so excited to talk to you both.'

'It's fine, honestly—and, actually, you called at exactly the right time.' Louis looked over at Santa. 'I was about to give Santa her present.'

She stared at him, her eyes wide with confusion. Wasn't all this her present?

'Here.' Reaching into the hamper, he pulled out a beautifully wrapped gift.

'Open it!' the boys chanted. 'Come on, Santa, open it.'

She pulled the ribbon, catching at the delicate paper. Heart thumping, she stared down in a daze. 'Oh, Louis…'

'Okay, we're going to go now.'

Glancing up, eyes burning, she nodded wordlessly at Kate as the screen went blank.

'You shouldn't have,' she said slowly, gazing down at the beautiful diamond necklace.

'I absolutely should. You're my wife.' He hesitated.

'I have a confession. It's not a new piece. It belonged to my grandmother. My grandfather gave it to her on their wedding day.'

It was difficult to speak past the lump in her throat. 'I can't accept this, Louis.'

'I want you to.' His eyes were steady on her face. 'Turn around,' he said softly.

Feeling choked, she reached up and touched the glittering diamonds. 'I don't know what to say.'

'You don't like it?'

He was teasing her—or maybe he wasn't. There was an intentness to his gaze, as if her answer mattered. As if he was asking another entirely different question.

She felt her lip quiver. 'Of course I do. I love it. I love—' She stopped herself just in time. 'I love everything about it. It's beautiful.'

He shook his head. 'Any jewellery can be aesthetically pleasing, but for me, it only comes to life when a beautiful woman is wearing it.'

He made her come alive, she thought, gazing up at him, her heart sliding helplessly free of its moorings. Only she could never tell him that.

But she could show him without words.

Clutching his shoulders, she pulled him closer, moaning softly as his mouth covered hers, her body turning boneless as she felt the hard press of his erection.

Later, they lay together, their limbs overlapping among the crisp white sheets. Pulling Santa's warm body more closely against his, Louis buried his face in her hair, breathing in her clean, floral scent.

He had wanted to give her a birthday to remember.

It felt like the least he could do after everything she had done for him. She had not just made him face the past. She had given him back a future he'd thought was lost. Given him back his home. His mother.

But it was more than that. Santa had given him back his self-esteem. When she looked at him, she saw the best of him. And in doing that she somehow loosened everything inside him.

Thinking back to the moment when he had told her about going fishing with his father, he felt his pulse slow. He'd spent so long alternately hating his father or blanking the past that he had forgotten those early mornings out by the water, but suddenly the memory was there, soft-edged and warm, like sunlight fluttering through a veil of leaves. His father's sudden, swift approval as he caught a fish, the measured instructions spoken in that quiet, authoritative voice.

His breathing stilled as he pictured Santa's expression. The softness in her eyes both astonished and scared him. Or maybe what scared him was how badly he wanted to stay here in this tower with her for ever...

'What are you thinking?'

He looked down at her, his head still reeling. But of course it was only natural that he would want to stay in bed with this beautiful woman, he told himself quickly.

'Nothing, really. Just that you have a very lovely family.'

She smiled. 'They're your family now too.' Her fingers tightened on his arm. 'Thank you for this. For everything.'

He glanced at his watch. 'Your birthday's not over yet.'

'I know.' She smiled. 'But it's not just my birthday.

It's Christmas Eve too. And that means that tomorrow will be Christmas Day. So I was thinking you might like to ask your mother over to lunch.'

Her eyes found his and he felt his heart stop beating. And then he breathed out shakily. 'I might just go and speak to her now.'

After Louis had gone, Santa sat on the window seat in the tower room, her eyes fixed on the roof of the Dower House that was clearly visible over the snow-topped hedges. She knew that things would be good between mother and son—she was sure of it.

It had taken a long time, but Louis had come home, and she was so happy for him. He was getting his old life back, but it would be a different life too—one with new possibilities.

Her heart squeezed. More than anything she wanted their marriage to be one of those possibilities—a marriage in which their vows were true. And that would mean telling Louis that she loved him. It would mean taking a risk—the biggest risk in her life. But what was marrying a stranger if not a risk? Surely what had happened in Klosters had taught her that in life, and in love, sometimes risks were meant to be taken.

She felt her pulse skip. They weren't strangers now. Nor were they the same people who had squared up to one another in Klosters. She was more rounded, less prickly and uncertain, and Louis was different too. That coiled-spring tension she'd assumed was part of who he was had disappeared, just like it did with her when she came off the ice after a competition.

'There you are.'

He was back, and her stomach flipped over as he

strode across the room and pulled her into his arms. Breathing in the scent of his warm skin, she rested her head against his chest, absorbing the steady stroke of his heartbeat.

'How did it go?'

'Good…' Releasing her, he joined her on the window seat. 'It's not like it was before. It's better. More honest.' His eyes found hers. 'She cried when I asked her to lunch. She was so happy.'

'So she's coming? That's wonderful. I'm so pleased she'll be there for your first Christmas at home.'

'Our first Christmas…' he said softly.

She felt her heartbeat accelerate. If she was going to say something it was now or never.

But before she could open her mouth to speak Louis said quietly, 'She showed me these scrapbooks my father kept. About me…about Callière. There were letters too. Letters he never sent, telling me how proud he was of me.'

She squeezed his arm. 'What matters is that he wrote them, and now you've read them.'

He nodded slowly. 'She gave me this, as well. She said he always intended for me to have it, but he was too proud to reach out to me. And what made him most proud was that I didn't come asking for it.'

He held out a piece of paper: a cheque. She stared down at it, stunned, her heartbeat stalling, her eyes juddering along the lines of zeroes. 'That's a lot of money.'

'I know—it's a crazy amount.' His eyes burned into hers. 'But it means I can buy out the shareholders. I'll finally own Callière.'

Holding herself completely still, she stared up at

him, a smile pasted on her face. Of course he should be happy. It was what he wanted more than anything. His prize. Only if he didn't need the shareholders' money then he didn't need to be married, and he didn't need her.

'Hey, don't look like that.' His hand tipped her chin up. 'Nothing's changed. I'm not going to renege on our deal. You don't think I'd do that, do you?'

Feeling sick, she shook her head. She knew he would stick to his word, but his word wasn't what she wanted any more. She wanted his heart. Only that wasn't on offer. The door she had thought was opening wasn't just closed, it was locked, and she didn't have the key.

She never would.

Knowing that made a hysterical bubble of panic fill her throat, and if it hadn't hurt so much she might have laughed.

It wasn't fair. She had thought pretending to the world that she loved Louis beyond reason would be hard, but to look into his eyes every day for a year and pretend she *didn't* love him would be an incomparable torture.

She wouldn't be able to conceal it. She wasn't even sure she could bear it. But she definitely couldn't bear it alone, and suddenly she wanted her family. She wanted to go home.

Only if she told Louis that, then there would be a scene. He would ask questions that she couldn't answer—or, worse, she might end up answering, and it would be mortifying for him to know the truth. Far better for her just to leave without a fuss. At least that way she might find it easier to let go.

'Of course I don't.' Her smile was aching now. 'We have a deal, right?'

A deal that felt like a vice around her heart.

CHAPTER ELEVEN

THAT NIGHT IN BED, she wrapped her arms around his neck, holding him close, trying to remember each quickening breath, trying to commit to memory every second of their last night together.

Afterwards, he fell asleep quickly and completely.

Holding her breath, she dressed in the darkness, and then picked up the bag she had discreetly packed earlier and crept downstairs.

The house was silent.

She had booked a taxi, and the man on the end of the phone had promised her that he would be there before midnight. It was now only half-past eleven, but she couldn't have stayed upstairs a moment longer.

Leaving her bag by the front door, she made her way to the drawing room. There was a good view of the drive, and although the fire was dying it still had a hot orange core. She stood in front of it, shivering. It was as if there was ice in her veins. She didn't think she would ever be warm again, and a part of her was glad. She wanted her heart to freeze and not to have to feel anything ever again.

'You know, you're supposed to be hurrying down the chimney tonight, not out through the front door.'

She turned, her heart hammering in her throat.

Louis was standing in the doorway in his pyjama bottoms. In the light from the fire the blue of his irises looked bruised, and his face was still and unsmiling.

'I'm sorry. I know you wanted me to spend the day with your mother, but I just can't do it.'

'Do what?' He walked across the room and stopped in front of her.

'Lie to her. I just don't think I can do that.'

'Why not? Why particularly not to her? We've lied to everyone else,' he persisted.

'Because she loves you.'

Because I love you.

She almost spoke the words out loud, but something in his eyes stopped her. All of a sudden it was as if none of it had ever happened. As if they had never kissed or made love. He was a cold, distant stranger.

'So you thought you'd just sneak out in the middle of the night? It's Christmas Eve, for—' He swore under this breath. 'And what about saying goodbye to Sylvia? The staff? My mother? What about saying goodbye to me? Could you not do that either?'

Striving for calm, she looked up at him. 'It's not goodbye,' she lied. 'We're going to see each other.'

He took a step closer. 'I'll take that as a no, then.' His eyes fixed on her face, cool and glittering like cut gemstones. 'Is this because of the money? The money my mother gave me? I meant what I said. I'm not going to cut you loose.'

'I know…you said. We had a deal and you're going to

stick to it. That's what we agreed, and nothing's changed between us, has it?'

The hope in her voice sounded deafening and her breath caught as he hesitated, seemingly on the point of saying something, but then he shook his head.

'No, nothing's changed, Santa. Nothing at all.'

Of course it hadn't. This was and could only ever be a marriage of convenience for Louis. Anything else was just her overreaching, just like she did out on the ice sometimes. Only this time she had a chance to pull back.

Swallowing past the lump in her throat, she said quickly, 'Look, I'm glad you sorted things out with your mum, and that she's going to be here for Christmas, but I want to go home. To see my family. And then I need to start training again. Obviously, we can still make public appearances together, like we agreed, but this seems like a good time for both of us to move on.'

There was a short silence, and for one beautiful, fleeting moment she thought it would be all right. She actually believed he would stride across the room as he had done earlier, pull her into his arms and tell her that he couldn't let her go, that he wanted her, needed her, loved her, and that she was essential to his life.

'I suppose it does,' he said slowly. 'You know, I actually thought you were different, Santa. I really did. But you're just like everyone else. This was always about you, wasn't it? What you want. Your needs.'

'That's not fair, Louis, we both wanted this—'

'Actually, I don't know what you want. I thought I did, but now I don't think I ever knew you at all. Goodbye, Santa.'

He turned and walked away, and Santa pressed her hand against her mouth, the tears she had been holding back spilling hotly down her cheeks as she grieved for the man she had loved and lost. The man who had never been hers to lose.

Louis stepped into the bedroom, his whole body shaking with shock and a pain like nothing he had ever imagined.

He had woken to find the bed empty, and at first he hadn't been concerned, only then he had realised that it wasn't just the bed that was empty but the room, and that Santa was gone.

Even then he hadn't thought she was *gone* gone, but then he had made his way downstairs and seen the bag by the door. He still couldn't believe it. He had never felt closer to anyone. Never trusted anyone so much. Needed anyone more.

Loved anyone more?

His heart stopped beating. That couldn't be true. He didn't believe in love. Marina had cured him of that particular myth.

Except he hadn't loved Marina.

His mother had told him that and she was right. But then she knew him better than anyone.

'You're like me—romantic,' she'd said. *'Your heart rules your head every time. But you're also stubborn, like your father, so that you can't see what's right in front of your nose.'*

His mother was right about that too. He hadn't seen what was right there in front of him, but Santa had.

Only now she was gone. It was too late.

* * *

Glancing up at the sky, Santa blinked. It was snowing again. Heavier than before. By morning, Waverley would be cut off from the world. But for her it would always be out of reach.

The thought almost undid her, and she stopped and swiped at the tears spilling down her cheeks. It was difficult to walk when you were crying. Harder still when your heart was breaking in two.

'Santa!'

For a moment she thought she was imagining it, hearing voices, footsteps crunching on snow. Only then, turning, she saw that Louis was there beside her, dressed now, his breath white in the air, his eyes blazing in the darkness.

'You have something of mine. You need to give it back before you leave.'

She sucked in a breath, hurt, horrified, the momentary flicker of hope that had flared in her heart instantly snuffed out.

'I didn't take your grandmother's necklace. I know how important it is to you and your family. I wouldn't do that. I left it upstairs.'

'I'm not talking about the necklace.' His voice seemed to stall in his throat, and then he reached up and touched his chest. 'I'm talking about my heart, Santa.'

For a moment she thought she must have misheard him. 'I don't understand—'

'You have my heart.'

She stared at him, deprived of both speech and breath, as his hands slid around her body and he pulled her closer.

'Ever since I met you I haven't felt like myself. I couldn't work out what was wrong with me. And then, literally a moment ago, I realised there was nothing wrong, and the only reason I didn't know what I was feeling was because I've never fallen in love before.'

Her heart was speeding now, heat blooming over her skin. 'You love me?'

Breathing out shakily, Louis nodded. 'I'm crazy about you,' he said softly. 'Completely smitten. And I'm sorry it took so long for me to realise that.' His arms tightened around her. 'I don't want you to leave. Not because of some stupid deal, but because I love you and I can't live without you.'

He looked down at her, everything he was feeling shining from his eyes. Framing his face with her hands, she kissed him fiercely. 'I love you too, Louis.'

As snowflakes fluttered onto their faces the sound of bells rang out across the blanketed fields and Louis pulled her closer. 'Happy Christmas, Santa baby,' he whispered, and then he kissed her.

EPILOGUE

ALMOST EXACTLY THREE years later, Santa stepped out of
the shower and wrapped a robe around her damp body.
Today was Christmas Eve—but it wasn't just Christmas Eve. It was Christmas Eve at Waverley, and a very
special private anniversary.

Obviously she and Louis celebrated their wedding
day, but this was the day when their marriage had
stopped being one of convenience and become instead
a marriage of love.

A love that had only grown stronger and more pre-
cious with every passing year.

Her heartbeat fluttered as she touched the delicate
diamond bracelet around her wrist. Louis had woken
her with breakfast in bed and a kiss—which, as usual,
had turned into passion. They had made love slowly and
tenderly, taking their time, letting their pleasure build
until neither of them had been able to bear it any more.

Afterwards he had given her this bracelet, but she
had decided to wait just a little longer before giving
him her gift.

She dressed quickly and made her way downstairs.

Louis was in the hallway, gazing up in satisfaction at the two immensely tall Christmas trees.

'You're not still gloating, are you?' she said, biting into the smile curving her lips.

He grinned. 'Definitely taller.'

She rolled her eyes. For some unfathomable masculine reason that she and Merry didn't understand, every Christmas Louis and Giovanni competed over who had the tallest tree. Last year Giovanni had won by an inch. This year Louis had trumped him by half a foot.

'I'm sure Giovanni has got more important things on his mind this Christmas. Like being a dad,' she teased. 'Besides, size doesn't matter.'

Louis pulled her into his arms. 'I think we both know that's not true,' he said softly.

She felt a prickling of heat dance across her skin as his blue eyes drifted over her face and down her body.

'But maybe if you're having doubts we should go back upstairs…'

Her stomach tightened, her breasts suddenly aching. She wanted to. Her need for him was as strong as his for her. But…

He groaned. 'I know, I know… I said I'd walk down to get my mother and I can't be late.'

Leaning into him, she kissed him slowly, hungrily. 'No, you can't be late. But there's always later.'

Louis stared down at her, savouring the hunger rising inside him. He truly believed he was the happiest man on earth. Marrying Santa hadn't just changed his life, it had changed *him*. And for the better.

He was stronger, calmer, kinder.

She had made him grow up and face his fears, and with her by his side he knew that anything was possible.

'Not too much later, though,' he said, sliding his hand through her hair and pulling her closer. He grimaced. 'Talking of my mother, I need to get Sylvia to help me wrap the portrait. You do think she'll like it, don't you?'

Looking at him, Santa nodded, her heart swelling. 'She'll love it.'

The painting was a surprise for the Dowager Duchess. The first official portrait of the Tenth Duke of Astbury and his Duchess.

'I still think you should have been wearing your medals,' he said.

She laughed. 'They're not that kind of medal.'

His blue eyes flared. 'Maybe—but you still earned them, and I'm so proud of you, baby.'

'I know.'

And not just proud—he had been so supportive. Waking early to come to the rink and watch her train, attending every round of every competition.

Her dream had come true. She had won gold and Louis had been there with her.

She felt her face grow warm. Maybe it was time to give him his present.

'But the painting is finished now,' she said.

He frowned. 'It can be changed. We can change it. Do you want to change it? I could call Andrew. He only lives thirty minutes away. I'm sure I could persuade him to drop round this afternoon.'

Her heart skipped a beat. She had been hugging her secret to herself since yesterday, dithering over when would be the perfect time to tell him. Now, though, she knew that there was no need to choose.

Every moment with Louis was perfect.

'That won't work…' She stood on tiptoe and gently kissed his beautiful curving mouth. 'The baby won't be here until June.'

* * * * *

Caught up in the magic of
The Christmas She Married the Playboy?
Don't miss the first instalment in the
Christmas with a Billionaire duet
Unwrapped by Her Italian Boss *by Michelle Smart*

Also check out these other Louise Fuller stories!

The Terms of the Sicilian's Marriage
The Rules of His Baby Bargain
The Man She Should Have Married
Italian's Scandalous Marriage Plan
Beauty in the Billionaire's Bed

Available now!

WE HOPE YOU ENJOYED
THIS BOOK FROM
H HARLEQUIN
PRESENTS

Escape to exotic locations where passion knows no bounds.

Welcome to the glamorous lives of royals and billionaires, where passion knows no bounds. Be swept into a world of luxury, wealth and exotic locations.

8 NEW BOOKS AVAILABLE EVERY MONTH!

#3969 CINDERELLA'S BABY CONFESSION
by Julia James

Alys's unexpected letter confessing to the consequences of their one unforgettable night has ironhearted Nikos reconsidering his priorities. He'll bring Alys to his Greek villa, where he *will* claim his heir. By first unraveling the truth...and then her!

#3970 PREGNANT BY THE WRONG PRINCE
Pregnant Princesses
by Jackie Ashenden

Molded to be the perfect queen, Lia's sole rebellion was her night in Prince Rafael's powerful arms. She never dared dream of more. But now Rafael's stopping her arranged wedding—to claim her and the secret she carries!

#3971 STRANDED WITH HER GREEK HUSBAND
by Michelle Smart

Marooned on a Greek island with her estranged but gloriously attractive husband, Keren has nowhere to run. Not just from the tragedy that broke her and Yannis apart, but from the joy and passion she's tried—and failed—to forget...

#3972 RETURNING FOR HIS UNKNOWN SON
by Tara Pammi

Eight years after a plane crash left Christian with no memory of his convenient vows to Priya, he returns—and learns of his heir! To claim his family, he makes Priya an electrifying proposal: three months of living together...as man and wife.

HPCNMRA1221

#3973 ONE SNOWBOUND NEW YEAR'S NIGHT
by Dani Collins

Rebecca has one New Year's resolution: divorce Donovan Scott. Being snowbound at his mountain mansion isn't part of the plan. And what happens when it becomes clear the chemistry that led to their elopement is still very much alive?

#3974 VOWS ON THE VIRGIN'S TERMS
The Cinderella Sisters
by Clare Connelly

A four-week paper marriage to Luca to save her family from destitution seems like an impossible ask for innocent Olivia... Until he says yes! And then, on their honeymoon, the most challenging thing becomes resisting her irresistible new husband...

#3975 THE ITALIAN'S BARGAIN FOR HIS BRIDE
by Chantelle Shaw

By marrying heiress Paloma, self-made tycoon Daniele will help her protect her inheritance. In return, he'll gain the social standing he needs. Their vows are for show. The heat between them is definitely, maddeningly, *not*!

#3976 THE RULES OF THEIR RED-HOT REUNION
by Joss Wood

When Aisha married Pasco, she naively followed her heart. Not anymore! Back in the South African billionaire's world—as his business partner—she'll rewrite the terms of their relationship. Only, their reunion takes a dangerously scorching turn...

---

*Rebecca has one New Year's resolution: divorce
Donovan Scott. Being snowbound at his mountain
mansion isn't part of the plan. And what happens
when it becomes clear the chemistry that led to their
elopement is still very much alive?*

*Read on for a sneak preview of Dani Collins's
next story for Harlequin Presents,*
One Snowbound New Year's Night.

Van slid the door open and stepped inside only to have Becca
squeak and dance her feet, nearly dropping the groceries she'd
picked up.

"You knew I was here," he insisted. "That's why I woke you, so
you would know I was here and you wouldn't do that. I *live* here,"
he said for the millionth time, because she'd always been leaping
and screaming when he came around a corner.

"Did you? I never noticed," she grumbled, setting the bag on the
island and taking out the milk to put it in the fridge. "I was alone
here so often, I forgot I was married."

"*I* noticed that," he shot back with equal sarcasm.

They glared at each other. The civility they'd conjured in
those first minutes upstairs was completely abandoned—probably
because the sexual awareness they'd reawakened was still hissing
and weaving like a basket of cobras between them, threatening to
strike again.

Becca looked away first, thrusting the eggs into the fridge along
with the pair of rib eye steaks and the package of bacon.

She hated to be called cute and hated to be ogled, so Van tried
not to do either, but *come on*. She was curvy and sleepy and wearing
that cashmere like a second skin. She was shorter than average and
had always exercised in a very haphazard fashion, but nature had
gifted her with a delightfully feminine figure-eight symmetry. Her

ample breasts were high and firm over a narrow waist, then her hips flared into a gorgeous, equally firm and round ass. Her fine hair was a warm brown with sun-kissed tints, her mouth wide, and her dark brown eyes positively soulful.

When she smiled, she had a pair of dimples that he suddenly realized he hadn't seen in far too long.

"I don't have to be here right now," she said, slipping the coffee into the cupboard. "If you're going skiing tomorrow, I can come back while you're out."

"We're ringing in the New Year right here." He chucked his chin at the windows that climbed all the way to the peak of the vaulted ceiling. Beyond the glass, the frozen lake was impossible to see through the thick and steady flakes. A gray-blue dusk was closing in.

"You have four-wheel drive, don't you?" Her hair bobbled in its knot, starting to fall as she snapped her head around. She fixed her hair as she looked back at him, arms moving with the mysterious grace of a spider spinning her web. "How did you get here?"

"Weather reports don't apply to me," he replied with self-deprecation. "Gravity got me down the driveway and I won't get back up until I can start the quad and attach the plow blade." He scratched beneath his chin, noted her betrayed glare at the windows.

Believe me, sweetheart. I'm not any happier than you are.

He thought it, but immediately wondered if he was being completely honest with himself.

"How was the road?" She fetched her phone from her purse, distracting him as she sashayed back from where it hung under her coat. "I caught a rideshare to the top of the driveway and walked down. I can meet one at the top to get back to my hotel."

"Plows will be busy doing the main roads. And it's New Year's Eve," he reminded her.

"So what am I supposed to do? Stay here? All night? With *you*?"

"Happy New Year," he said with a mocking smile.

Don't miss
One Snowbound New Year's Night.
Available January 2022 wherever
Harlequin Presents books and ebooks are sold.

Harlequin.com

Love Harlequin romance?

DISCOVER.

Be the first to find out about promotions, news and exclusive content!

Facebook.com/HarlequinBooks

Twitter.com/HarlequinBooks

Instagram.com/HarlequinBooks

Pinterest.com/HarlequinBooks

YouTube.com/HarlequinBooks

ReaderService.com

EXPLORE.

Sign up for the Harlequin e-newsletter and download a free book from any series at
TryHarlequin.com

CONNECT.

Join our Harlequin community to share your thoughts and connect with other romance readers!
Facebook.com/groups/HarlequinConnection